THE HORRIBLE TERRIBLES

THE HORRIBLE TERRIBLES

For more information: artbydiego.com/contact

First paperback edition October 2024

Cover design by Driss Chaoui

Library of Congress Control Number: 2024921452

ISBN: 979-8-9917452-0-8 (paperback)

ISBN: 979-8-9917452-1-5 (ebook)

www.artbydiego.com

THE HORRIBLE TERRIBLES

DIEGO BARRIENTOS

Publishing

To Connor. Thanks for the band name and memories, bud.

"Because no battle is ever won he said.
They are not even fought.
The field only reveals to man his own folly and despair,
and victory is an illusion of philosophers and fools."

—William Faulkner, *The Sound and the Fury*

———

"A day without sunshine is like, you know, night."

—Steve Martin... probably

1

THE HORRIBLE CAR

CARLOS GARCIA ONLY NEEDED TO SHAVE HIS FACE FIVE TIMES during his entire deployment. At 21, he barely passes for 18. His thin frame gives him the illusion of height, but standing next to others often provokes the joke, "Do your parents know you're here?" The remark still annoys him. After a year in the Iraq War, and three years away in total, he has finally set foot back in California: Fort Irwin, an army base stranded in yet another desert.

To welcome the soldiers home, fire trucks parked near the runway spray arcs of water over the buses transporting them from the plane to the ceremony—a grand, surreal return to reality. The welcome home ceremony had been energetic, full of speeches and awards for the families' entertainment while Carlos could only think about going home.

He stands by the curb outside the Welcome Center, his two green duffle bags and backpack by his side, still in his least damaged uniform, itching to change. His remaining uniforms are either stained by oil and grease or so severely sun-bleached that his superiors can't make out the camouflage pattern. The one he's wearing was deemed worthy of the ceremony, as it only has a small tear on the right knee.

He adjusts his collar and boonie hat, the fabric rough against his freshly buzzed head, a reminder of the year spent in them. What a year. Three hundred and sixty-five days of wearing a hot, unbreathable uniform despised by the locals.

Carlos watches as other soldiers around him reunite with relieved parents and eager partners, disregarding his presence. His own parents had gone to get the car, leaving him alone to wait. He avoids eye contact with the PDA as he fiddles with his backpack zippers. The scents of perfume and cologne, which he hasn't smelled in months, mix with the exhaust fumes from the parking lot.

His parents pull up in a shiny new Ford Explorer, a clear contrast to the old, worn-out Buick LeSabre they used to have. His mother waves from the passenger seat, a smile on her face. His dad gives a nod from behind the wheel.

"You didn't tell me about the new car," Carlos says, trying to mask his surprise as they load his bags into the back of the SUV. "Thanks," he adds, climbing into the back seat, the scent of leather hitting him.

"Cool, huh? We got it a couple weeks ago and thought we'd surprise you," his dad says, his chin lifted.

"Wait till you see the new house!" his mom chimes in. She reaches a hand back from the front seat, squeezing Carlos's knee.

"Yeah," he says, the words flat. Carlos shifts his gaze out the window, his stomach sinking as a familiar feeling settles in— the one that's followed him through seven elementary schools and three high schools. This time, his family moved while he was away, informing him only through a phone call.

They pull out of the parking lot and begin the three-hour drive back to Bakersfield. Carlos stares out the window, admiring the scenery—a distinct kind of desert. Proof the army hadn't just flown him in circles for twenty hours, convincing him he was in the Middle East. The color of the dirt is darker in California, with some dark green sprinkled out over yellow hills and interesting rock structures that spark memories of high school road trips during which these natural desert towers served as familiar beacons.

"That was the happiest group of people I've ever seen," his dad laughs. "And those trucks! Were those the ones you guys used in Iraq?" He eyes Carlos in the rearview mirror.

"No, those fancy ones stay there for training. We used the armored ones that the unit we replaced over there had used. Then we left them for the unit that replaced us. Pieces of shit, really."

"Well, the new house is brand new. No one has used it before," his dad announces with a proud smile.

Carlos nods, trying to muster enthusiasm. "That sounds great, Dad. The photos were nice."

A moment of silence follows, filled only by *Led Zeppelin III* playing on the car stereo as the desert turns to farmland. They pass an almond farm selling nuts along the highway—Carlos remembers visiting here as a kid. His mom twists around in her seat to look at him, her eyes warm and loaded with emotion.

"Nice to have you back, *mijo*," she says.

"Thanks, Mom." Carlos gives her a smile.

"So you're like, done-done now, right?" His dad's voice is a mix of curiosity and relief.

"Oh yeah. Totally out," Carlos answers, feeling a sense of finality in his words.

His mom's eyes search his face. "What are you gonna do next? College?"

Carlos shifts uncomfortably, staring out the window as they approach Bakersfield. "I mean, yeah, eventually. Right now home is next. I haven't been left alone in a room in forever." His voice trails off, memories of the barracks and the constant presence of his friends flooding his mind. Even being alone in a port-a-potty was off limits. Once a soldier entered one, a constant stream of practical jokes ensued. Like dropping rocks through the roof vent.

CARLOS STEPS out of the car and takes in the new neighborhood. The few teenaged trees planted along the street are still bare from winter even though it's starting to get warm already. Not all the houses are complete—some only wooden skeletons reminiscent of the blown-out buildings during the war, and others with fresh stucco walls.

The neighbor's house is nearly finished, and the construction workers, done for the day, flock to their trucks. Spotting Carlos's uniform and duffle bags, a few of them give him a quick salute. Their boots puff clouds of dust into the air in a way Carlos can relate to. They leave tan footprints that stand out on the fresh black asphalt. Carlos casts his eyes around the neighborhood, taking it in again. Bakersfield is known for its constant construction of new homes, but there isn't a single thing for entertainment in sight.

The brand-new single-story white house with dark green trim feels alien. This is the first time his family has owned a new house. He grew up in apartment complexes and a double-wide mobile home, moving into their first house when he was a senior at his third high school. That last house had peeling, faded blue paint, a dented garage door, and one of the windows had thick plastic duct-taped to the outside from the time someone threw a rock through the glass.

Carlos's mom steps out of the car, stretching her back. "It's nice, right? Clean and peaceful."

"Yeah."

His parents help him carry his belongings into the garage. Carlos takes a deep breath and then heads to his new room. As he enters, he notices his parents have tried to decorate it like his old room. The artwork and knickknacks reflect outdated interests and tastes—music he's outgrown and skateboarders who no longer inspire. The only comforting item is his drum set, though it's clear his dad, who never played, assembled it. The setup is awkward and unfamiliar.

He sits on the edge of his bed, taking in the room. The walls are bare except for the few outdated posters, and the furniture is sparse. He feels a pang of nostalgia for his old room, despite its imperfections.

His mom peeks in, smiling softly. "We tried to make it feel like home," she says.

Carlos smiles. "Thanks, Mom. I appreciate it."

His dad joins them, wiping his hands on his jeans. "Need any help setting up the drums? I tried," he laughs.

"Nah, I got it. I just need some time to get everything right."

"Alright, let us know if you need anything," his dad says, patting him on the back.

They leave Carlos alone in his new space. He stands up and changes out of his uniform into some Vans, skinny jeans, and a faded blue NOFX t-shirt, then examines himself in the mirror. He lets out a quick chuckle as he sees a leaner, tan-lined version of his older self... until his eyes meet his left hand, which is now scarred and missing a pinky. He ran over a roadside bomb two months into the deployment, but luckily it was a smaller one. The explosion only destroyed the heavily armored truck's door and drivetrain, but the heat from the blast got Carlos's left side and burned his hand since his small window was open and his hand was resting on the door. He remembers the explosion vividly—the sudden jolt, the searing heat, and the disorientation that followed.

He reassembles his drums the correct way, adjusting each piece until it feels familiar again. Putting on his headphones, he pulls out his iPod—the same iPod that survived the blast with only a slight burn mark across the screen. Without hesitating, he selects blink-182's *Enema of the State*, the album that inspired him to join his first band.

He starts to play. Despite the missing finger, he quickly adapts, using a new hand technique he's been practicing. There's no pain, only awkwardness at first. The sound of the drums echoes throughout the house, filling every corner with energy. The rhythm courses through him, each beat a reminder of why he loves music. His eyes remain closed and his whole body is into it. As if he's playing in front of thousands of people.

2

THE TERRIBLE JOB

FOR THE FIRST TIME, CARLOS HAS HIS OWN COMPUTER IN THE house. No more sharing the family one that ties up the phone line like before he left. His family pitched in and got him a laptop before he deployed to Iraq. Myspace and AIM ended up being the best ways to communicate with them while he was away. The lines to use the phones on base were often over an hour's wait, and international phone cards were expensive.

He lounges on his bed, watching his new favorite YouTube channel—someone named Tara Wheeler posting live footage of bands around Bakersfield. The quality is impressive compared to most live band videos he's seen. Hours pass as Carlos exhausts all of Tara's content.

He checks his Myspace post announcing his return from deployment and, to his surprise, finds a message from an old high school friend, Houston. In his profile picture, Houston is playing bass in a garage, stirring a subtle thrill in Carlos. They haven't spoken since their graduation party, but they quickly arrange to catch up over an early drink.

. . .

CHUY'S MEXICAN Grill is a popular spot with vibrant colors and the enticing aroma of carne asada and grilled chicken filling the air. It's become Houston's go-to spot. Carlos makes his way to the patio area, where he sees Houston already seated, sipping a beer and smoking a cigarette. He's calm and steady, with a short beard and a faux hawk, dressed in a flannel shirt and jeans.

"Hey!" Houston shouts from his seat, raising his beer in a casual salute.

Carlos waves at Houston but makes a detour to the outside bar to order his beer before taking his seat. The lively chatter and clinking glasses create a buzzing atmosphere. He approaches the bartender, who barely believes his ID.

"This is my first time ordering beer from a bar here," Carlos says, joining Houston.

"At Chuy's?" Houston asks, smoothly putting out his cigarette into the ashtray between them.

"No, I mean like, ever," Carlos smirks. "Well, I mean in the civilian world. I've ordered beer on base near El Paso. It was eighteen and older there."

"No shit? That's wild. So how was it over there?"

"It was alright," Carlos laughs. "Just glad to be out now. I was very over it..." His smile straightens.

"Well, glad you're back. Lots has changed."

"Yeah, I saw you got married! And you're a dad! How's that going?"

"It's alright," Houston jokes, mocking Carlos's casual response. "I miss a lot of stuff if we're being honest. But overall it's good for me, man. I don't drink as often anymore."

"Well, that's good. You still playing bass?" Carlos asks.

"Yeah, but not like, seriously. I've got the kid now, and work, so that takes up most of my time."

Carlos's lips tighten into a thin line, a corner lifting in an attempt at a smile as he looks down at his drink.

"I still jam, though," Houston continues. "With a couple of guys from work every once in a while. What about you? Are you still playing?" His eyes drop to Carlos's hand. "Oh shit, dude, your hand. I'm sorry, that was rude."

Carlos laughs. "It's all good. I mean, we have to talk about it. At least it's not my face."

"Yeah. Or your hair. Are you gonna grow the 'fro again?"

"Yes! It can't grow out fast enough."

"You still playing drums, though? Like, *can* you?"

"Yeah, totally. It doesn't hurt that much anymore. I never use my pinky or that side of the hand when playing anyway." Carlos attempts to shrug it off but can't hide his disappointed tone.

"Dude, you should apply to Best Buy. I'm a supervisor there now. Everyone there is in a band. Maybe you'll find one."

"Yeah, that does sound cool."

"That's it! You're applying online tonight. Tomorrow I'll find your application and go from there."

"Are you serious? That would be fantastic, thanks."

"Of course," Houston says with a paternal smile.

Carlos lets his mind drift as they continue reminiscing about high school and family life. The familiar rhythm of Houston's voice brings back vivid memories of youthful mischief.

"Well, I'm getting another," Houston says, rising from his seat. Carlos watches him make his way to the outdoor bar, weaving easily through the clusters of people enjoying the evening. The bar is a lively place, filled with conversations and the occasional burst of laughter.

When Houston returns, he's carrying two more beers. Pulling a couple of water bottles from his pockets, he sets them down on the table with the beers with a nod.

"Thanks, but I think I'm good with this one," Carlos laughs. "I'm already pretty buzzed."

"I thought the army bulked you up?" Houston asks.

"Not in that heat."

"Three beers for me, then." Houston pauses. "What else is new with you?"

"Nothing at all," Carlos laughs. "Been watching a lot of live music on YouTube. There's this channel, Tara Wheeler, who shoots local bands. Ever heard of her?"

Houston nods. "Yeah, Tara's cool. She's at almost every show, filming. You should check out Gerry's Pizza sometime. That place is busy now."

"No shit? Gerry's?"

"Oh, yeah," he says as he checks his watch. "Hey, I gotta get home before the kid goes to sleep." Houston finishes his beer and wipes his mouth with his sleeve. "Could I get a ride?"

"Sure thing," Carlos agrees. He finishes his water in two chugs and they head home.

FOLLOWING HOUSTON'S ADVICE, Carlos sits at his laptop that night, the screen casting a blue glow over his face as he fills out the job application. Each question feels like a reminder of the time he's lost—far from the mundane rituals of civilian life.

Lying in bed later, he can't help but wonder how different things might have been had he not missed those three years of his life to the army. Would he have stayed in Bakersfield? Or stayed in his old band? Would his friends still be alive? Would they have been killed regardless? His mind races, the silence of the night amplifying his thoughts. The nights are the hardest.

HOUSTON FOLLOWS through the following afternoon and hooks Carlos up with an interview with the assistant manager at Best Buy. Two days later, Carlos arrives at the store wearing a blue tie, a white button-up shirt tucked into his black Dickies, and black shoes.

He meets Houston and the assistant manager by the entrance next to Loss Prevention, and together they walk through the bright, bustling store, the sounds of different departments blending into a song. They make their way to the conference room in the back, located near the bathrooms and break room, trying to avoid being stopped by lost customers.

Inside the conference room, Carlos shifts slightly in his chair, the leather creaking softly beneath him as the interviewers exchange quick, assessing glances. When he begins to answer their questions, his responses are steady, his military discipline evident. The confidence in his voice is almost unexpected, as a brief, muted discussion follows, ending with the assistant manager's approving nod.

"Congratulations, you've got the job," she says with a smile. "You'll be in the camera department."

Houston grins. "You can start today if you want. You don't get the blue polo until you're done with your probation period, so what you're wearing now is perfect. Just lose the tie. Gabi Rosales is there now, she'll show you around."

Carlos nods, feeling a combination of relief and excitement. He follows Houston to his new department, taking in the layout of the store as they walk. When they arrive, he spots a young woman wearing the traditional blue polo tucked into her tight khakis, dusting a large Canon DSLR camera. Her long, thick, dark brown hair is loosely tied in a ponytail.

"Gabi, this is Carlos," Houston says, introducing them. "He's starting today."

"Hey, Carlos," she responds with a loud smile.

"Hello," Carlos says as he feels a flush rise to his cheeks.

"Alright, I gotta go. Let him shadow you, Gabi." Houston disappears around the corner.

As Gabi guides Carlos through the small, circular camera

department, they chat and get to know each other. The counters displaying various cameras form a neat perimeter around the space, with the cash register situated at the center like a hub. As they walk the inner circle, she pauses occasionally to adjust a display, her movements fluid and confident.

"Where'd you work before this?" she asks. Her dark, warm, almond-shaped eyes draw Carlos in.

"I actually just got out of the army. So I guess this is my first job."

"Second job then, right?"

"Yes, second I guess."

"I didn't want to be a dick and assume you're training to be a cop. 'Cause of your hair."

"That's right, I forget," Carlos laughs. "I can't even hide if I change clothes. I hate it. I usually have long curly hair and I miss it so much."

"Hair grows back. Until then I'm hiding my weed from you, though." They laugh. Carlos can't stop appreciating her smile. Her teeth are unnaturally straight and white. She continues, "So, the army. Are you a killer?"

"Wow, straight to the big one. No, I'm not. Wasn't that kind of war."

"What do you mean?"

"Never fired my weapon once, but was attacked all the time." He shows her his scarred left hand.

"Jesus. But did you *want* to fire your weapon?"

"I mean, I wanted to defend myself and my friends, yes. But I wasn't like 'I can't wait to kill someone.' You ask a lot of hard questions for just meeting somebody."

"I need to know who I'm working with."

Gabi turns to greet a customer who's come into the department. Carlos follows and shadows her to learn. He's never worked retail before and he knows he should be paying attention to the interaction, but instead he finds himself trying to think of what to say to Gabi next. He blushes as he realizes he's been staring at her for way too long, hoping nobody noticed. The customer leaves.

"I don't want people to see 'army' when they first see me. I want them to see 'artist,'" Carlos voices his rehearsed thought.

"I want people to see 'Mexican' when they see me, but I always get 'Asian.'"

"Damn." Carlos lets out an awkward chuckle.

"But OK, I get it now. Long curly hair would do wonders." They laugh together. "So, you're an artist? That's cool, me too," she says, her face glowing. "What do you do?"

"I'm a musician. I play drums. What about you?"

"I'm a photographer."

"Right on. Like, to be in galleries or to be in like, magazines?"

"Museums and history books are more like it."

"My bad. You're a dreamer too," Carlos smiles.

"Hasn't happened yet, obviously," she says, gesturing at the duster by the register. "But I love photography. Landscapes, people, anything really. Even taking photojournalism classes. That would be a great day job."

"Right on. I guess there's a lot of vets out there now, but I've never met another one who also wants a career in the arts. So the last few years have been kinda lonely."

"Well, it's your lucky day, Carlos the Artist. My boyfriend's a veteran too! He got out a year ago, and he plays guitar. His name's Jake."

"Oh, cool." He tries to hide the disappointment in his voice and focus on the intriguing prospect of meeting a fellow veteran musician.

"Yeah. Hey, we're going to a show at Gerry's on Saturday. You should come. I'll introduce you two."

"Sure, that sounds great."

3

THE HORRIBLE MUSIC

THAT SATURDAY NIGHT, CARLOS ARRIVES AT GERRY'S PIZZA downtown on Gabi's invitation. He parks down the street and walks past several closed storefronts where homeless people huddle under dirty blankets in the nooks next to boarded-up windows. The sidewalks are littered with old gum stains and trash, yet the smell of street tacos and beer overpowers everything else.

As he walks, memories of Iraq surface unbidden. The boarded-up windows and makeshift shelters echo the environment he left behind. He quickens his pace, trying to shake off the complicated memories, focusing instead on the familiar aroma of pizza signaling the approaching Gerry's.

The smell pulls him back to the present. The streets here, despite their grime, offer a sense of normalcy, a far cry from the war. Carlos takes a deep breath, letting the scents and sounds of home anchor him, even as the memories linger at the edge of his mind.

Downtown Bakersfield has a completely different vibe than the rest of the city. Remnants of the Old West town it used to be are noticeable behind the bail bonds, check cashing, and the only remaining mom-and-pop restaurants. He used to love coming here as a kid. The rest of Bakersfield is an ocean of track homes and fast food chains.

Carlos arrives and takes in the Gerry's Pizza sign. Gerry's was once known for being lousy with cockroaches; he wonders if that reputation still holds. Either way, it's now the most popular local music venue in town. A beautiful refuge for the people who don't want to be associated with the rest of the strongly Christian and conservative town.

He enters through the front and pays the five-dollar cover. The place has a small stage in the basement, and the space can hold about a hundred people. If someone were to come in through the artists' entrance, which is in the back of the space furthest from the stage and leads to the alley, they would never know there is a small restaurant with a bar above.

Carlos heads down the stairs, searching for Gabi. The stairs to come down to where the concert-goers hang out are just to the right of the stage, so people crowd them to get a closer look at the acts.

As he descends, a short and wider guy in a dark blue hoodie bumps hard into his shoulder, causing Carlos to jostle against the sticky handrail.

"Sorry," Carlos mutters, but the guy continues up the stairs, oblivious. He runs a hand over his shaved head, sighs, and continues down the stairs, feeling out of place.

The opening band is setting up their gear, so it isn't noisy yet. Most of the people are still outside or ordering pizza upstairs before the music starts.

"Carlos!" Gabi yells as she spots him first.

"Hey!" He walks toward the back of the space where she's hanging out, and she gives him a warm hug. The young man standing next to her is smiling but eyeing Carlos warily, so Carlos fights the urge to linger in the hug. The guy is tall, with dark, untamed wavy hair just hiding his ears, and is dressed like he's about to take the stage. Black waxed jeans that have never been washed, an even blacker long-sleeve waffle shirt, and worn, black, minimal leather boots. Despite his young face, Carlos can't help but notice there are faint signs of stubble—evidence that he needs to shave more often than Carlos does.

"Jake, this is Carlos, who I was telling you about," Gabi introduces them.

Jake is quiet for a second; then a teasing grin lights up his face. "How can you play drums without a pinky?"

"Turns out I don't really need it. I have more stamina now. Less mass to move."

Jake laughs and extends a hand. Gabi rolls her eyes with a chuckle and turns toward the stage.

Carlos watches Gabi for a moment while she's distracted by Jake, who is pointing out the amps used by the opening act with his other arm around her. Her hair is no longer in a ponytail, and she is dressed in a black tank top and jean shorts with long black tights underneath. He shifts his gaze, feeling the need to focus on anything else.

The band starts playing, so the conversation stops. It's a local act made up of what appears to be high schoolers. They are opening up for the touring band coming in from L.A. that Gabi and Jake like. Carlos has never heard of either.

The basement of Gerry's is dark and already humid from the dozens of music fans jumping and pushing each other, and from the ovens upstairs. There are no windows, but a breeze from the open front door makes its way down the stairs and out the open artists' entrance in the back, relieving some of the heat. The benefit of it not being packed yet.

The walls of the basement are made of crumbly brick, probably here since Prohibition days, but there's a barrier of long-haired, black-clad wallflowers in case someone gets shoved into the sharp edges. The lead singer of the band, without the burden of an instrument, takes advantage of the metal pipes firmly attached to the ceiling. They're low enough to grab onto and lean into the front of the crowd.

The teenage band finishes playing, and Carlos, Gabi, and Jake head up the stairs and out the front for some air before the next band starts. The night is cool, and a light breeze carries the murmur of voices. About thirty people are outside, smoking cigarettes and talking about the opening act.

Jake glances at Carlos's scarred hand. "So, you using your GI Bill soon or what?"

"My parents want me to," Carlos replies. "I mean, that's one of the reasons I joined, but I think I wanna be in a band. That's the dream. I mean, if those kids can do it..." he laughs.

"It's always gonna be there. That shit don't expire," Jake says. "Have you been in a band before?"

"Yeah, a few before the army. Now I just jam to my iPod."

Jake nods. "You should come over to my place tomorrow. My folks are barbecuing. We can talk music afterward."

Carlos grins. "Sure, that sounds great." Gabi peers over at both of them and smiles.

4

THE TERRIBLE MEDALS

CARLOS PULLS UP TO JAKE'S HOUSE FOR THE BARBECUE, HIS HANDS tightening briefly on the steering wheel. He scans the unfamiliar front yard, lingering in the car a moment longer than necessary before stepping out. The thought of meeting the parents of someone he just met feels heavy, but Jake's mention of music flashes in his mind, and maybe that's enough for now.

He steps out, taking in the distinct architecture and meticulous landscaping. As he approaches the towering dark wooden door with intricate carvings, he straightens his shirt. The door swings open, and Jake stands there, smiling, his shoulders relaxing at the sight of Carlos.

"Sweet, you're here," Jake says, though Carlos senses an underlying tension in his voice. "My dad's already being a dick." Carlos can hear a male voice yelling in the background.

They make their way through the house toward the backyard, where Jake's dad has two grills going, cooking ribs and tri-tip. The grills and picnic table are under an awning next to their dark blue pool. Seeing Carlos, Jake's dad straightens and his mood changes.

"Hey there, Carlos. Thank you for your service." He extends a giant hand. "Welcome to Casa Robbins! Hope you're hungry."

"Hello. I am, thank you," Carlos says, shaking his hand.

He gestures to Carlos and Jake to take their seats. As they sit down at the picnic table, Jake's mom comes out with two glass dishes of potato salad and mac and cheese to join the meat. She says grace, and they begin to eat.

"Jake, aren't you hot in that long sleeve?" Jake's mom asks.

"It's not made of wool," he replies, a hint of irritation in his voice. "It's also February. I'm going out after this."

Jake's parents start reminiscing, telling Carlos stories about Jake's good grades in school, his early involvement in the church, soccer, and his military service. Jake's fingers tap a restless rhythm on the picnic table.

"Guys, can we not?" he mutters, voice low but strained.

"Why are you ashamed about serving your country?" Jake's dad asks. The table falls silent for a moment.

"What do you think about that Wounded Warrior program, Dad?" Jake asks, his tone sarcastic. "I think it's amazing how they're raising all this money for those not addicted to heroin... or homeless."

His dad's face tightens. "I don't want to start, Jake."

"Now you're shy?"

"Focus on something meaningful... like your music."

Jake scoffs. "Here we go."

Jake's dad shifts his focus to Carlos, his tone changing to one of admiration. "Now, Carlos here served our country honorably. It's something to be proud of, especially considering your background."

Carlos feels a knot tighten in his stomach. He knows what's coming next.

"You know, with your ethnicity and all, it must have been tough," Jake's dad continues. "But you did it. You proved everyone wrong."

Jake's face flushes with embarrassment. "Sorry, Carlos. I thought he would behave today."

"What? He did something meaningful," his dad says defensively.

"Let's just enjoy the barbecue, OK?" Jake's mom tries to intervene.

"I've spoiled you." Jake's dad ignores his wife.

"With what?" Jake spreads his arms wide.

"Stop talking to me like that, dammit."

Finally, Jake stands up, his chair scraping against the concrete. "Come on, Carlos. Let's just leave. I wanted to show you something anyway."

"Nice to meet you two," Carlos says before leaving.

He follows Jake inside, the argument still ringing in his ears. They retreat to Jake's room, where posters of bands and a couple soccer players cover every inch of the walls. Guitars are propped up alongside a keyboard and an old wooden harmonium, adding to the cluttered, musical chaos.

"Sorry about outside," Jake says. "Thanks for coming, I didn't wanna do that alone."

"No worries, I get it. Your dad was in the army, too, huh?" Carlos asks.

"Three generations of grunts," Jake responds, showing him his military shadow box, filled with medals and memorabilia from his deployment. There are sun-bleached uniform patches, a pack of Arabic cigarettes, an Iraqi army bayonet, a chalk-white desert rock with a dark core, and the generic deployment medals.

Jake stares at Carlos's scarred hand. "So, Purple Heart, huh? What was your MOS?"

"88M. Hauled fuel all over Iraq."

"Lucky," Jake says, fixing his eyes on the shadow box once again.

"Really?"

"Yeah, man. I wanted to fight. *Patriotism*, if you'd asked me why four years ago. Only did prison guard duty, though. Or boring tower guard." Jake shrugs.

Carlos lifts an eyebrow and tilts his chin. His eyes narrow slightly, searching for understanding.

"Yeah. You fuckers got all the action being out there on those roads all the time."

"It's not like I got to fight back." Carlos shakes his head. "They attacked us with IEDs, mortars, rockets, and snipers. Only defense was listening to music and driving on."

"I never got to fire my weapon," Jake sighs.

"Me neither, is what I'm saying. I just wanted to be a citizen and the whole college money thing. There was a ceremony after basic training where a bunch of us got naturalized. It was really cool," Carlos says, examining the old wooden harmonium and running his fingers over the worn keys.

Jake plays some music from his iPod docking station and picks up his guitar. He sits on his bed and doodles along with the song.

"I love The Used," Carlos says.

"Me too. Saw them when I was in high school," Jake responds without looking up from his fretboard.

"Lucky! I wanna see them so bad." Carlos begins browsing Jake's CDs.

"How long have you been playing drums?"

"Since I was two. My dad is a musician, so we always had at least a guitar lying around. But of course, I wanted to bang on stuff. So I got a Muppet Babies drum kit from Toys 'R' Us for Christmas when I was two."

"Muppet Babies, nice. My dad hates that I'm a musician. He thinks I'm a communist. If it wasn't for the pool and that he hasn't made me pay rent yet, I'd hate it here."

"I don't pay rent either. Thank God. I just started at Best Buy and I can already tell the pay's not enough for anything."

"At least it's not the oil fields," Jake says, still focused on his guitar.

"Oh, fuck the oil fields. I don't care how much that pays," Carlos says as they laugh. "I'd rather live in a car than risk my sanity working 14-hour days collecting oil for someone else."

"Why don't we start a band? You on drums and me on guitar?" Jake asks.

"Hell yeah, let's do it. Funny you played The Used 'cause I love that sou—"

"I'll post a flier and set up a location for rehearsal. I've been thinking about this for a while now. I already have a band name." Jake pauses, grinning. "The Horrible Terribles."

"OK, cool," Carlos says, laughing at the satirical band name. Feeling a bit timid after being interrupted but eager for this band to happen, he decides to go with it, and excitement fills him as he thinks about this new possibility.

5

THE HORRIBLE PIZZA

"Gerry, this is Carlos, the drummer I was telling you about," Jake says, nodding toward the burly owner of Gerry's Pizza. Carlos waves as he takes a seat at the bar. Gerry nods from down the counter, his permanent scowl softening a bit.

Jake, working as the bar back and pizza maker upstairs, hands Carlos a bottle of beer, glancing over at Gerry for permission. He approves with a thumbs up.

"Where's the flier?" Jake asks.

"Printed it at work," Carlos replies, pulling a large manila folder from his backpack and placing it on the scratched wooden counter. He takes a sip of his beer.

"OK, great. So what do you think, Gerry? Could we use the basement then?"

"Fine," Gerry responds. "I'll have to make you a key for the mornings. And only if I get a cut of your merch. CDs, shirts... even stickers."

Jake smirks at Carlos. "Sweet deal, right?"

Carlos's eyes widen as he nods. "Yeah!"

Jake smiles, then returns to work. Carlos enjoys his drink in his untucked blue Best Buy polo, taking in the environment as

Jake finishes his shift. The air is thick with the smell of baking dough, beer, and sweat. Upstairs, only a handful of older patrons linger, while the sounds of a band performing downstairs echo through the space. A show is happening tonight in the basement, drawing a lively crowd.

Carlos spins his stool and leans back against the bar, watching Jake weave throughout the space, collecting the empty glasses scattered around the bar while waiting for the pizzas to bake. The music from downstairs beats in Carlos's chest, a rhythmic thump that provides enough background noise for the drunks who tolerate it for a drink. The pizza is good too, so people still show up.

Carlos's mind drifts between the present and memories of drinking liquor, smuggled in through the mail, with his friends on old picnic tables in Iraq. The beats of the music are oddly comforting, like a heartbeat that grounds him. He catches glimpses of Jake moving among the tables, his face focused.

The music swells, vibrations traveling through Carlos's feet. Amidst the noise and smell of pizza, he feels a rare sense of belonging.

His stomach growls, reminding him he hasn't eaten since morning. His mom's text about what she made for dinner gnaws at him. "Thanks for the beer," Carlos says as he takes his last chug. "But I'm fucking beat, I think I'm gonna head home. Keep me posted!"

"Will do," Jake says without taking his eyes off his task. Carlos exits through the front door, leaving Jake behind the bar.

JAKE TAKES his last pizza out of the oven, the cheese bubbling and golden brown. He unties his apron and hangs it on a hook by the oven. Heading to the sink, he washes his face and tousles his hair with water, then puts on his black leather jacket. "Alright, Gerry, I'm heading out," he calls over his shoulder, grabbing the folder Carlos brought. Gerry nods as he writes in his log.

Jake makes his way downstairs, the sound of the band performing tonight growing louder as he descends. He opens the folder and tapes the flier that reads THE HORRIBLE TERRIBLES IS LOOKING FOR MUSICIANS: GUITAR, BASS, VOCALS NEEDED on the wall in the back of the venue by the bathrooms. The flier has little tearable phone numbers at the bottom. He steps back to make sure it's straight, then heads for the artists' entrance door at the back that leads to the alley.

Outside, the cool night air hits him, a welcome relief after the heat of the venue. An RV towing a white trailer with a bunch of stickers on it is parked near the door. He stops to look at them, recognizing a few band logos among the colorful mess. As he's examining them, he gets mobbed by two kids waiting by the door. "Can we have your autograph?" one asks, eyes wide with excitement.

"Uh, sure!" he answers, smiling. He doesn't correct them, letting them think he's someone famous. Jake dresses like he's in a notable band already, with his carefully curated outfit and careless hair. He signs the CDs the kids think he played on, his signature quick and fluid. The kids thank him and run off, giggling. Jake smiles.

He begins to walk toward the main street where his car is parked. The alley is not very long but sparsely lit, shadows stretching and shifting as he moves. Before he gets to the end, a figure steps out from behind a dumpster. Moving quickly, a man with brown teeth and an old green field jacket that hangs loosely on his frame shoves Jake against the wall with a knife. "Give me your wallet and phone," he shouts, jamming the knife against Jake's neck.

Jake's heart races as he fumbles for his things. The man

snatches them and runs off, disappearing around the corner. Anger and frustration boil over as Jake kicks at the debris around the nearby dumpster and yells. He grabs a piece of broken pallet and beats the dumpster with it, the noise echoing through the alley.

Breathing heavily, he drops the pallet and leans against the wall, trying to calm down. He heads back inside and upstairs to tell Gerry, who listens to Jake's story with a shrug. "That's rough, kid," he says, sliding a slice of pizza across the bar. "Here, nothing grease can't fix."

6

THE TERRIBLE AUDITION

CARLOS SITS BEHIND HIS DRUMS ON THE SMALL STAGE IN GERRY'S basement, his scarred hand gripping the sticks as he plays along with whoever steps up to audition. The stage is cluttered with cables and gear, including Jake's extra little combo amp and Carlos's dad's combo bass amp, so people coming to audition only need to bring their guitars. Gabi sits in a folding chair facing the stage, taking notes for Jake as he leads with his guitar alongside Carlos.

The basement glows yellow with the three light bulbs trying to fill the space. The scent of pizza and old beer waft through the air. The stage is small but elevated, giving the auditions a sense of importance.

After a few lackluster performances, off-key singers, fumbled notes, stiff fingers, and someone who brought sheet music, a young woman with sun-bleached strawberry-blonde hair framing her round face walks down the stairs with two guitar cases. She's dressed similarly to Carlos, wearing Vans, skinny jeans, and an Ataris t-shirt. There's an air of confidence about her that immediately grabs everyone's attention.

"Hi," she says. "I'm Michelle Cernan."

"Hey," Jake grins, giving her a nod. "I'm Jake, this is Carlos, and over there is Gabi. She's here helping out today."

"Hello, Michelle," Gabi smiles, jotting down her name.

"The Horrible Terribles, what a funny name. Whose idea?" Michelle asks.

"That'd be Jake." Carlos gestures at his bandmate.

"Alright, let's see what you've got," Jake asserts.

Michelle plugs in her guitar, her fingers moving with practiced ease. Carlos watches her closely, falling into the rhythm as they begin the jam. Her confidence is infectious, and soon the room is filled with a vibrant energy that had been missing before. Carlos admires how comfortable she looks on stage. After jamming for a few minutes, they stop to chat.

"Wow, you guys went to Iraq? You're not looking to start a country band, are you?" Michelle asks, grinning.

"No America porn, please," Jake groans.

"We love pop punk and Motown!" Carlos says with an enthusiastic nod.

"Oh, nice," she laughs. Her striking eyes are large, with the round, rich green of the iris fully visible. "I love that stuff too." She plays a simple, repetitive, yet catchy riff reminiscent of a loud nursery rhyme until a striking young man comes down the stairs from the restaurant. He is dressed in a similar style to Jake, but wears a tweed newsboy hat that barely fits over his thin dreadlocks that hang down to his sharp jaw, and his arms are collaged with small tattoos.

Michelle stops playing to greet him. "Oh yay, Gene, you made it!" Her eyes light up. "This is Gene Aldrin. Can we play you guys a song we wrote? He's a singer."

Jake tilts his head to the side, concerned. "You two aren't dating, are you?"

Michelle steps back, making space for Gene as she laughs. "We're not each other's type."

Gene opens one of the cases Michelle brought and grabs a guitar, slinging it over his shoulder. "I'm the voice," he jokes.

Carlos, seated at his drum kit, adjusts his grip on the drumsticks and nods at Michelle, ready to follow her lead. As she strums the opening chords, he jumps in with a steady beat, his heart racing with excitement. He glances up from his kit, a broad grin spreading across his face as he locks eyes with Gabi and Jake.

Gene's voice isn't what Carlos expected. It's not polished or conventionally pretty. He misses a few notes here and there, but his voice is loud, confident, and full of raw attitude. There's a unique edge to it, a distinct brand that catches Carlos off guard. He and Gabi are impressed, their heads dancing to the rhythm.

Jake, however, doesn't look sold.

As the song comes to an end and the last note fades, Michelle steps forward, her stance firm. The three leave her and Gene on stage to have a quick discussion on the staircase.

"Michelle's in," Jake whispers. "That song was fucking awesome. But Gene? Not so much."

"Come on, Jake," Carlos says, wiping sweat from his brow. "They've got something unique."

"Yeah, they do," Gabi adds, glancing at her notepad. "Gene's voice is different, but it stands out. Also, how many more people are you guys gonna check out? That's eleven guitarists, two bassists, and three singers."

"If you want me in the band, Gene's part of the deal. We're a package," Michelle yells from the stage. The three turn to look at her, surprised. "I can hear you guys," she laughs.

Carlos glances at Jake, silently pleading. Jake sighs, knowing he's outnumbered but feeling the weight of his decision. "Fine, but Gene plays bass. No one decent has come in for it anyway."

Carlos's excitement is evident in his smile. He glances at Jake, who clenches his jaw, just like during the argument at the barbecue. Carlos shakes off the tension he feels at the sight. Despite the unease, the four-piece band they've dreamed of is finally complete. A chosen family.

7

THE HORRIBLE ART

IN BAKERSFIELD, THE TWO BEST PLACES TO VIEW ART ARE THE galleries on either of the two college campuses: Bakersfield Community College, where Gabi is studying art and photography, and the state university. On this particular Saturday, Gabi is excited to finally take Jake to an art show at her college. She eagerly chats about the new exhibition, showcasing her extensive knowledge about the local art scene, photography, and its history.

As they walk through the bustling campus toward the gallery, Gabi shares, "You know, my parents weren't thrilled about me staying here for the first two years. 'It's cheaper than attending a university for the same gen-ed classes,' I told them. Plus, I get to experience the music scene here... and you, of course."

Jake forces a smile. "Yeah, sounds smart."

Gabi's eyes sparkle with excitement. "Being around the leading figures in my field is important, but living in the moment matters just as much."

"Totally," Jake mumbles.

They arrive at the gallery and start browsing the art. The

modest campus gallery is filled with vibrant artwork and a buzz of creative energy. Gabi leads him through the exhibit, pointing out her favorite pieces and explaining the techniques and stories behind them.

They stop at a large photograph, purposefully overexposed, titled *Planned Paradise (Death of Diversity)* by an artist named Evie Davis. The image is of a sprawling cookie-cutter neighborhood under construction, with partially built houses in various stages of completion. Wooden frames and exposed beams are prominently visible.

"The photo is kinda basic, right? Just a bunch of houses being built. But that title opens up so much information," Gabi explains. "And the overexposure just looks cool."

Despite her enthusiasm, Jake nods but finds his attention drawn to the painting next to the photo. It depicts a vast, dimly lit room with high ceilings, reminiscent of grand Baroque architecture, complete with intricate moldings and large arched windows that let in soft, diffused light. In the middle of this enormous space, there is a small, solitary figure sitting on a simple wooden chair. The figure appears dwarfed by the grandeur of the room.

"What's wrong with you?" she asks sharply, noticing his distraction.

"Gene and Michelle are doing more than just playing lead guitar. I just... don't want to be forgotten."

"Jake, the band's solid. Your dream of a four-piece is real now! And you got a songwriter, too."

He frowns. "But what if people like them more?"

Gabi's patience wears thin. "Can this not be about you right now? This was supposed to be fun for me too."

"Well, damn, Gabi, it's not like your work is in this show."

"What's that mean?"

"You're getting upset that I'm not jumping up and down over some paintings and photos."

"I'm upset 'cause I've been talking to myself this whole time."

Their voices rise, the argument heating up. Suddenly, a voice cuts through the tension.

"Gabi!" Both turn to see a young woman waving enthusiastically. Her tight, curly short blue afro shines under the lights, and her outfit—a white t-shirt tucked into black shorts, with black fishnet stockings and colorful enamel pins adorning her black suspenders—stands out.

Gabi forces a smile. "Perfect timing," she whispers, though there's still a trace of the earlier tension in her voice. The young woman runs up and gives her a warm hug. As they step apart, Gabi turns to Jake. "Jake, this is Tara Wheeler. We took a photography class together last semester. She only took the one class, though, while I'm here all week." Gabi gives Tara a playful jab on the shoulder, but her gaze flicks back to Jake, the unresolved argument hovering in the background.

"Well, I have other shit to do, you suck-up." Tara reciprocates the punch.

"Hey," Jake says, still quietly upset.

Gabi continues, "Tara has a pretty popular YouTube channel now where she posts videos of local bands."

"OK, OK, you can stop now... OK, keep going," Tara laughs. "Hi, Jake."

"You film bands?" he asks, his face lighting up.

"Yeah! I put little mics on the bill of my hat and film with my camera," she explains. "Gabi tells me you put together a band. How's that going?"

"Yeah," he responds. "The Horrible Terribles. You should film us."

"Oh! I saw a flier. You guys are opening Saturday for Senses Fail, right?"

"At Gerry's, yup."

"I'm already going. Sure, I'll film you guys."

8

THE TERRIBLE STAGE

As HE SCANS THE NEARLY EMPTY BASEMENT FROM THE BACK OF the stage, Carlos's palms begin to sweat, the weight of expectation pressing down on him. The musty smell of spilled beer fills the air, mixing with the faint scent of cigarette smoke from outside. The Horrible Terribles are the opening act on a four-band bill, with just enough rehearsed original songs to fill their fifteen-minute slot.

Their first rehearsals felt raw but promising. Michelle arranges the music, Gene handles the lyrics. Jake adds his lead guitar when Michelle hasn't already written one, and Carlos slams his drums behind them to create a sound that is full, energetic, and catchy.

Carlos sets up his kit with nervous urgency, feeling the pressure of time. He can't find his tuner, so he tightens the loose nuts by hand. It's a makeshift solution, and in the end he has to settle for out-of-tune drums, adding to his stress.

The small crowd, mostly familiar faces, makes it worse. Every reaction is visible, every glance feels personal. There's no way to blend in or disappear into the background. He can see every emotion, and there's nowhere to hide from the crowd's reactions, intensifying his sense of exposure.

Senses Fail, the headliner, is the main draw for the audience that hasn't yet filled the basement at Gerry's. Regardless, the room still buzzes with anticipation, and the faint hum of amplifiers creates an undercurrent of sound.

Gabi stands near the stage, camera in hand. She adjusts her lens, focusing on Carlos's scarred left hand, capturing his nervous energy as he adjusts the height of his crash cymbal. Houston, with a group of Best Buy employees Carlos vaguely recognizes, mingles at the back. A few members of the following bands who are leaning against the brick wall make up the rest, showing support.

Carlos glances up. Michelle is quiet, focused, and steady as she tunes her guitar with expert fingers. Gene cracks jokes, making the small crowd laugh as he adjusts the strap to his bass.

"Guess we're really packing them in tonight," Gene says with a wry smile. "Next time we'll just play in my mom's living room—she'd even make cookies." This earns a few chuckles from the audience. The jokes, silly as they are, calm Carlos. He chuckles too, and the tension in his shoulders eases.

Jake leans his guitar against his amp, weaving through the small, crowded stage, and jumps down. He joins Gabi, who is taking candid photos of the people leaning against the brick wall. Their easy banter adds a layer of normalcy to the chaotic pre-show setup.

Nearby, Tara adjusts her hat, a modified baseball cap with two little lavalier mics attached to the brim. She mutters under her breath as she checks the sound and light, her fingers deftly adjusting the settings. Her eyes are sharp and focused, scanning the stage with the practiced eye of someone used to capturing the perfect shot.

Gerry comes down the stairs, stopping halfway, and points

at his watch. The sight of his stern expression sends a jolt through Carlos. Jake notices and quickly jumps back on stage, taking charge and rallying the group to their spots.

"Let's go," he says, looking at Carlos to start the count-in.

Carlos grabs his sticks and glances at the audience. He takes a deep breath, feeling the slick of his sticks in his sweaty hands. His eye catches Tara's camera, and she gives him a thumbs-up. His stomach tightens, thinking of her YouTube channel and how many people might see this. Houston chats with his friends, pointing toward the stage and nodding in approval. Gene checks his mic. The crowd's expectant murmur grows louder. Michelle glances at Carlos, raising her eyebrows as she waits for his signal. He nods, trying to push down the anxiety gnawing at him. He clicks his sticks together.

They launch into their first song, but Carlos starts playing the wrong one, causing the rest of the band to look back in panic. The crowd winces. Michelle locks eyes with Carlos, questioning him. Jake, looking exasperated, raises his arms and waves them sharply, signaling everyone to stop. Michelle shifts her weight onto one foot, her annoyed gaze now boring into Jake.

Carlos swallows hard, his mouth dry as he shakes his head and lets out an involuntary nervous chuckle. He counts them back in, the clicks of his sticks echoing in the dead silence. They restart, this time all coming in together on the same song. His initial mistake lingers in his mind, affecting his focus. Each crash of the cymbal and boom of the bass drum feels heavier, like he's trudging through desert sand, slowing the whole band down. The crowd's mild applause after each song feels more like polite obligation than genuine enjoyment.

Carlos glances at Gene, who tries to lighten the mood between songs, but his humor barely penetrates the now-heavy atmosphere. Gabi catches Carlos's eye from the front of the stage, but her encouraging smile does little to ease his self-consciousness.

Tara films steadily, her lens frequently drifting toward Gene's face as he sings. Gene's casual charisma and stage presence make him a natural focal point; his every gesture is effortless. Jake's eyes flicker between Tara and Gene, his posture tightening with each glance.

Carlos's coworkers shout his name and make rock 'n' roll gestures as the band finishes their last song, their enthusiasm standing out in the otherwise subdued crowd. Their voices rise above the muted clapping, trying to infuse some energy into the sparse applause. Despite the supportive shouts and gestures, the overall response from the audience is lukewarm.

"WE SHOULDN'T HAVE RESTARTED. We should've just followed Carlos's lead," Michelle argues as she unplugs her gear.

"Restarting means Tara can easily edit a clean set. She can cut out the mistake," Jake counters, putting his guitar in its case.

"I'm sorry, guys," Carlos apologizes again as he takes apart his drums.

"You did fine," Gene says, clapping Carlos on the back. "I've done worse."

Carlos forces a smile, but his mind races with self-doubt. The Best Buy crew approaches the stage.

"Hey, man, that was awesome!" Houston says, a broad smile on his face. He gives Carlos a fist bump.

Jake straightens up, guitar case in hand. His eyes narrow as he watches the interaction, and he clears his throat. "We've got a week till the show at the Gate."

The Best Buy group exchanges glances, then begins to back away.

"OK... later, Carlos," Houston says as he and his friends walk up the stairs.

"Thanks for coming, guys," Carlos waves back.

"I'm also working on booking us at the Mint," Jake continues, bringing Carlos back into the conversation with his stare. "So come on, Carlos."

"Couldn't find my goddamn drum key. Couldn't tighten anything. I got in my head," Carlos explains.

Michelle and Gene nod, their expressions a mix of exhaustion and seasoned acceptance. Carlos is the last to pack up. His drum set, a modest dark green four-piece, still takes time to disassemble. He moves quickly, detaching cymbals and folding stands as the next band starts bringing their gear onto the stage. The others have already disappeared into the night with their lighter loads.

He pauses, staring at the spaces on the stage where they'd been, now swallowed by strangers. A familiar loneliness creeps in. The sting settles in his chest, sharper than he expected. He tightens his grip on the last cymbal stand, telling himself to keep packing up.

9

THE HORRIBLE BREAK

"BUT I DROVE ALL THE WAY FROM LAKE ISABELLA FOR THIS!" A middle-aged, skinny man with deep-set eyes exclaims in Carlos's face. His breath is hot and reeks of coffee and cigarettes. His sun-aged skin peels slightly around his nose. "Your website said you had it in stock."

Carlos feels the heat of the customer's frustration radiating off him, his own patience wearing thin. He takes a deep breath, trying to maintain his composure. The fluorescent lights above seem to hum louder, adding to the commotion. "I'm really sorry for the inconvenience, sir. Sometimes our inventory updates don't reflect real-time stock. I can check with our nearby stores or order it for you onlin—"

"There's another Best Buy in Bakersfield?" The customer's voice sharpens with sarcasm, his eyes narrowing. "I needed it today. This is ridiculous."

Carlos forces a polite smile, though his teeth clench under the weight of the customer's glare. "I understand, sir. Let me see what I can do."

The customer storms off, muttering under his breath. Carlos watches him go, the tension in his shoulders easing slightly. He sighs and rubs the back of his neck, feeling the strain. Taking a moment to glance around, he notices the buzzing activity throughout the store. Customers are scattered in various sections, examining laptops, smartphones, and televisions, while the overhead PA system replays the same pop song Carlos has heard five times today already. At the center hub next to Carlos, Gabi is ringing up a camera for a couple, her wide smile and enthusiastic chatter marking her as a natural saleswoman.

Carlos goes back to restocking camera cases from a shopping cart brought over by the warehouse crew. The repetitive motion of organizing the shelves helps calm him down since it doesn't require speaking to a customer. The circular camera department, with its meticulously-arranged displays of DSLRs, video cameras, and point-and-shoots, always feels like a little oasis in the midst of the chaotic store.

As Carlos reaches for another box, he catches sight of Jake entering through the sliding doors. Straightening up, he watches him weave between the DVD and cellphone departments. Jake's shoulders are slightly hunched, and his eyes are glossy.

Jake heads straight for Gabi, who is still busy assisting the couple. "Hey, Jake," Gabi says warmly, giving him a quick hug while still maintaining her attention on the customers. "I'll be with you in just a sec, OK? I need to help these people real quick."

Jake nods, his eyes darting around the store. Gabi turns back to her customers, her focus now split between them and Jake. While he waits, Jake wanders over to Carlos, trying to seem casual.

"Hey, man," Jake says, his voice lacking its usual energy.

"Hey. You alright?" Carlos senses something is off.

Jake glances at Carlos's tense posture. "What's up with *you*? You look like you just got chewed out."

Carlos sighs. "Just had an asshole customer. Drove all the way from Lake Isabella, only to find out the thing he wanted is out of stock. Not a happy guy."

"Why would someone drive all that way without calling first? What did he want?"

"A memory card." Carlos shakes his head. "What are you doing here?"

"Here for Gabi's lunch break. I was bored at home..." Jake's voice trails off.

"You sure you're OK?"

Jake looks around, making sure Gabi is still busy. "Well, I was off today and was just lying in my room, bored as fuck. The TV was driving me crazy, so I shut it off and lay there in silence. That's when my tinnitus kicked in again. Suddenly, I was back in Iraq, in that goddamn guard tower. Bored out of my mind, exhausted, but having to keep my eyes open to scan my zone." He rests his hand on the back of his neck. "Then my dad knocked on my door, and I jumped. It snapped me out of it, but hiding that reaction from him made me so mad I spiraled. After he closed the door, I lost it. I couldn't breathe for a moment. Like I was stuck in an elevator. I don't even remember why he came in."

"Damn, dude. Have you talked to anyone?" Carlos asks, concern in his voice.

"A few months ago, yeah. But they just throw pills at you," Jake replies, shaking his head.

"They gave me pills, too," Carlos admits. "What kind?"

"Don't tell Gabi," Jake says, his tone firm.

"About the pills?"

"No, about the episode."

"Why not?" Carlos presses.

"Just don't, OK?" Jake insists, avoiding Carlos's gaze.

Just then, Gabi returns, having finished with her customers. Clearly noticing something amiss between the two of them, she raises an eyebrow. "Hey, is everything OK? The vibe here feels a little weird."

Carlos quickly glances at Jake before responding. "Yeah, everything's fine. Just an asshole customer earlier."

Jake nods in agreement. "Nothing to worry about, though. Carlos handled it like a pro."

Gabi looks between them. "OK, if you say so. By the way, Carlos, they're talking about you in my earpiece. Houston may come find you."

"Of course," Carlos laughs.

"Lower enlisted always get blamed and never praised, am I right, Carlos?"

Carlos nods and smirks.

"This isn't the army, boys. Houston won't scream. Just wants to know what happened 'cause *he* got yelled at."

"So... like the army?" Jake continues to tease.

Gabi tilts her head and puts a hand on her waist, then looks at Carlos. "Now that it's slow, I'm gonna take my thirty. Be back."

"Where you guys eating?" Carlos asks.

"Quizno's," Jake says.

"Ol' Reliable, huh?" Carlos laughs. "See you in a few."

Gabi and Jake head toward the exit, the atmosphere between them lightening as they leave the store. As Carlos watches them go, he feels a tap on his shoulder and turns around to greet Houston.

"So," Houston starts. "Your first asshole."

"We were out of stock," Carlos says as he puts a camera case back into the shopping cart. "So I offered to order it, but—"

"Don't worry about that. I think you pissed him off 'cause you were so chill. He probably thought you were mocking his anger," Houston laughs. "People like that want magic. He can learn to use the internet."

"You handle these cases a lot, huh?"

"We're in corporate retail, dude," Houston laughs again. "Don't change who you are." He pats Carlos on the back and exits the circular enclosure.

Left alone in the camera department, Carlos goes back to restocking the shelves, glancing behind and around him for customers with nervous anticipation.

10

THE TERRIBLE LEADERS

DRIPPING IN SWEAT, CARLOS PACES THE BASEMENT AT GERRY'S TO catch his breath while Jake, Gene, and Michelle rest on their amps. The space feels lived-in, their gear arranged with the ease of frequent use. The echo of their last song lingers in the air, mingling with the scattered empty water bottles, discarded setlists, and the distinctive blend of herbal throat-coat tea and the tang of body odor.

At Gabi's suggestion, the band now practices every weekday morning before its members head to work, taking advantage of the closed and empty space. Jake's deal with Gerry still stands, regardless of how often they practice—as long as they're out by the time the place opens for lunch. When it does, they move their gear to an unused storage room. Recently, Carlos proposed that anyone who can sing should also sing backup vocals, so they've added an electric kettle and boxes of tea to their inventory.

Gabi and Tara descend the stairs from the restaurant above, their unexpected arrival catching the band off guard. Tara carries a box of donuts, while Gabi has her camera in hand.

"Perfect! We're just now breaking," Jake says as Gabi snaps his photo.

"Wow, it smells in here," Tara says, scrunching her nose.

"Like gold records," Gene jokes.

"Thanks for the donuts, guys," Carlos says, grabbing a chocolate bar from the box.

Tara places the box of donuts on the stage and the rest attack it.

"You guys are gonna throw up when you start to play again," Tara laughs. "We'll be outside." She and Gabi step out through the artists' entrance together for some relief from the stuffiness, leaving the band to eat.

THE AIR OUTSIDE in the alley is refreshing despite the late summer heat, a welcome change from the muggy basement. Gabi and Tara find a quiet, shaded spot near the side of the building next to a dumpster.

"Fuck, it's hot out." Gabi pulls the bottom of her shirt out to let the air flow in. "That breeze, though."

"I hate the summer here." Tara leans against the wall, taking a deep breath. "So, how's school going?"

"It's going alright. I'm working on my transfer applications. It's a bit stressful, but I'm excited. Just wondering what it'll mean for me and Jake."

Tara nods, a thoughtful look on her face. "That's a big step. Have you talked to him about it?"

"Not really," Gabi admits. "I don't want to distract him."

"You should talk to him," Tara says, her voice soft. "Sounds important."

Gabi nods.

Tara sighs, glancing up at the sky. "I wish I had something like that to focus on. My dad's being an ass as usual, and I'm just fucking bored."

"What's he doing?"

"Basically, he hates our neighborhood and takes it out on us instead of the assholes. I guess I get it. Living in a place where the only things whiter than the neighbors are the whites of their eyes when they stare and judge."

"Jesus."

"Yup," Tara says with a sarcastic grin. "And to top it off, he's threatening to cut me off if I don't do something with my life."

Carlos swings open the artists' entrance door. "Hey, you guys want in on this weed? Gene brought his bong."

"In a minute."

Carlos nods and walks back inside.

THE AIR in the basement is already thick with the lingering scent of weed. Carlos sits back on his drum throne and puts his sticks away in the bag strapped to his floor tom. Gene walks over and hands him an elaborate, green-and-orange-swirled glass bong. He takes a rip.

The trashy air from the alley followed Carlos inside, mixing with the weed and body odor. Michelle and Jake sit on their amps, fiddling with their muted guitars.

"What's been your favorite venue?" Gene asks Carlos as he returns the bong.

"Besides Gerry's?" Carlos says as he exhales. The smoke swirls under the yellow light bulbs. "I really liked Sandrini's. Super fun drunk crowd. Although it felt like they preferred covers."

"The Gate for me," Michelle adds, taking the bong from Gene. "The sound engineer kills it every time, every band."

"You just wanna fuck her," Gene jabs.

"OK, yes. But she can also be good at her job." Michelle tries not to laugh as she exhales.

"No other than Gerry's for me. Feels like home," Jake says, taking his turn.

"You don't get sick of this place?" Carlos asks.

"Gerry's more supportive and a better cook." Jake lets out a plume.

"Does he let you sleep in here, too?" Gene asks, taking the bong from Jake and placing it in front of Carlos's bass drum.

The door swings open as Gabi and Tara enter, letting in the sharp sunlight for a moment. Their eyes sparkle with enthusiasm as Tara gathers everyone's attention. "Guys, we have an idea," she starts, her voice full of conviction. "I think I should manage the band. With Gabi."

Carlos and the others stare back at them with blank, unfocused eyes.

"Tara's videos of bands performing on YouTube have gotten the attention of L.A., and she has a lot of free time and a passion for music," Gabi adds.

Carlos snaps out of it and leans forward from his drum throne, wiping sweat from his forehead. He notices the same sudden realization from the others. Gene nods eagerly, and Michelle, sitting on her amp, gives a thumbs-up.

But Jake crosses his arms, a frown deepening on his face. "Why you, Tara?" he asks, his voice laced with suspicion.

Tara doesn't miss a beat. "You guys have been playing around Bakersfield for like, what, six months now? Your Myspace is barren. Do your fans even know Gerry's is your home base? Have you played L.A. yet? Plus, you guys need someone who isn't just another musician, or in the band, to steer this ship. You guys can focus on creating and performing."

"And I'll take photos and make sure you guys get paid after the show," Gabi says.

"There's money in this?" Gene jokes.

"We've been doing fine without a manager. I've been booking shows," Jake retorts, his tone defensive.

"But now they're contacting *us*. Probably because of Tara's videos," Michelle counters. Jake's shoulders tighten.

Gene steps in, his voice calm but firm. "I don't know, man. I think they've got a point. We could use the help, especially with L.A. gigs and getting our name out there."

Carlos tilts his head at Jake, understanding his point of view, but seeing the potential benefit of Tara's proposal. "Jake," he says. "This sounds pretty sweet. Let's give them a chance."

The room falls silent, all eyes on Jake as he wrestles with his pride. Finally, he exhales sharply. "Fine," he mutters, "but if this doesn't work out, we go back to the way things were."

Carlos feels a mixture of relief and apprehension. The others nod in agreement, sealing the decision. Tara and Gabi are now officially the band's managers. Michelle and Gene embrace while Jake gives Carlos a quick smile before pulling Gabi aside.

"Gabi, what the fuck?" Jake whispers.

"What?" she responds, confused.

"What about what we talked about at the gallery?"

"I thought this was a great idea. Are you honestly gonna tell me you don't think she'll be great for the band? People know her. She knows people."

"But we're fine with me as leader right now."

"Jake, lose the ego for a moment, would you?"

"Fine," he says after a pause.

"Love you," Gabi fishes.

"Love you too."

"Jake!" Gerry booms from the stairs. "You working today or what?"

"Coming!" Jake yells back.

"See you after work," Gabi says as Jake kisses her.

"Later everyone, I gotta work," Jake says as he leaves.

"See ya!" Carlos calls from behind his drums, gathering the broken sticks scattered across the back of the stage.

"I've got some mushrooms. Who's up for camping?" Gene asks.

"Let's go!" Carlos shouts. "But I gotta be back before my shift tomorrow. I open Saturdays."

"You two have fun with that," Gabi laughs.

"I'm heading home," Michelle says, giving everyone a warm hug before heading up the stairs. Tara wraps an arm around Gabi as they follow her. Carlos and Gene make plans as they put away their equipment.

11

THE HORRIBLE TRIP

CARLOS AND GENE STOP BY THEIR HOUSES TO PICK UP CAMPING gear and then head out toward the hills east of Bakersfield, past Tehachapi. The sun dips lower in the sky as they drive, casting long shadows over the landscape. They arrive with an hour's worth of daylight left, finding a secluded spot that overlooks a vast, rugged valley.

"Perfect," Carlos says, stepping out of the car and stretching. The air is cooler up here, a welcome change from the day's heat.

Gene grins, already beginning to unload their gear. "Yeah, this'll do."

They work in companionable silence. Carlos gathers rocks and arranges them in a circle, methodically creating a safe space for their fire. Meanwhile, Gene sets up his portable iPod speakers on a flat rock, making sure it's all connected and charged.

"Got any requests?" he asks, looking up from his task.

Carlos winces. "I hate being DJ."

Gene laughs and selects an album. Soon, the opening chords to the Descendents album *I Don't Want to Grow Up* fills the air, blending with the sounds of nature around them. Carlos finishes the fire pit and takes a moment to appreciate his handiwork.

"Oh, yeah," Gene says, coming over to inspect the pit. He pats Carlos on the back. "We make a good team."

Carlos chuckles. "Yeah, we do. Let's get that fire going."

They gather wood, and soon a small fire crackles to life, its warm glow pushing back the approaching darkness.

Gene leans back on his arms, propping himself up from his seat on the dirt. His eyes close as he lets the music and the fire's warmth wash over him. "What is it about fire? This is exactly what I needed."

Carlos nods, staring into the flames from his seat. "Me too, man. Me too."

Gene leans up, grabs a few pills from his backpack, and takes them. "Oh, don't worry," he says, noting Carlos's expression. "I have asthma, diabetes, and, um..." He pauses, shifting his position slightly. "Anxiety."

"What anxiety meds?" Carlos asks with concern.

"Klonopin."

"Me too. Check it out," Carlos giggles, grabbing his own from his backpack to show Gene. "Jake takes these too. What gives you anxiety?"

"Family issues. And basically being gay in the black community. Especially in Bakersfield. What about you?"

"I guess Iraq, but I don't know. I feel like always moving around growing up and never really having a home has something to do with it too."

"Yeah, that sucks. But, hey! Mushrooms." Gene takes out the bag. "We're here to celebrate."

They take the psychedelics and start to dance around the fire pit. Soon the music seems to settle into their bones. The flames flicker, casting interesting shadows across their faces.

They exchange glances, small smiles playing on their lips, feeling a shared, wordless understanding.

Carlos feels the initial euphoria wash over him, a wave of intense joy and exhilaration that makes his heart race and his senses sharpen. The colors around him seem brighter, the sounds clearer, and the rhythm of the music pulses through his body with an almost electric intensity. He laughs, a spontaneous burst of happiness that feels like it's bubbling up from the core of his being as he dances around the fire with Gene, their movements wild and uninhibited.

But as he admires the fire, as quickly as it came, the euphoria begins to wane. The vibrant colors and sharp sounds start to distort, twisting into something darker. The heat around the fire grows hotter, more menacing. His heart races and a wave of panic washes over him. He stumbles back, away from the fire, and sits down heavily on the ground, trying to steady his breathing.

Gene notices immediately and turns down the music. He crouches beside Carlos, his face filled with concern. "Hey, man, you OK?"

Carlos shakes his head, trying to control his rapid breathing. "I... I can't breathe."

Gene rummages through his backpack and pulls out a small bottle. "Here, take this," he says, handing Carlos an anxiety pill. "It's only an anxiety attack. Bad trips are usually just anxiety."

"Thanks," he musters as he takes the pill with trembling hands, swallowing it dry. He focuses on Gene's voice, grounding himself in the present.

"What do you do if this happens and you're sober?" Gene asks. "Follow my breaths." Gene begins breathing slowly, holding his breath at the top of his inhale and the bottom of his exhale. Carlos follows and starts to calm down. "Good, keep following my breaths." Carlos's shoulders drop and he starts to breathe normally again. "Are you OK?"

"Wow. Yeah, I'm feeling better. That breathing pattern works?"

"Yeah, man. Box pattern. My therapist taught me that."

"I last did mushrooms in Iraq with my best friend. Maybe this was too soon to take them again," Carlos explains. "He was killed in the war in an explosion. I only lost a finger in *my* explosion, so I can't help but feel guilty for being alive now."

Gene stares at him with a mix of surprise and curiosity. "You guys ate mushrooms in Iraq?"

"That's your takeaway?" Carlos chuckles, shaking his head.

"That's a dark story, dude. I'm sorry for your loss. That has to suck." Gene places a hand on Carlos's shoulder, his grip firm yet reassuring. "But in case you forgot, you're on mushrooms. Gotta keep you laughing," he jokes, making Carlos laugh. The tension eases from his body. They stand up, still laughing, and begin to skip around the fire pit again. Carlos feels his trip becoming easier to handle, but then a small aftershock of anxiety reveals itself.

Gene notices Carlos's momentary unease. He turns down the iPod again and gestures for Carlos to sit beside him.

"My family has PTSD," Gene says, breaking the silence. "Not from any wars or anything, but I get it."

Carlos takes a seat next to him, grateful for the understanding.

Gene continues, "Some advice: stay away from alcohol. The family members I have that have come through to the other side all say the same thing. That shit slows down the healing and only hurts the ones around you."

Carlos nods.

"I've seen it." Gene watches Carlos begin to tap on his knee with his scarred hand and shake his leg. "I can drink, though.

Not you," he says, making Carlos giggle. "Just stick to the natural shit, though, seriously. Weed and mushrooms."

"A *little* bit of mushrooms. And some Klonopin," Carlos teases.

"Yes! Mustn't forget."

"So, you and Michelle? You guys met in high school, right?"

"Yeah, in high school. Well, summer school. Our dumbasses had to make up classes every summer. The second summer we recognized each other and laughed. Started talking and found out we had a lot in common." Gene looks into the fire with an intense gaze, as if those long-ago days and memories are flashing before his eyes. "Both queer, similar family drama, both love music. She basically forced me to play guitar. I only wanted to sing at first."

Carlos feels much more relaxed now that the medicine has finally kicked in. He settles down in his sleeping bag while Gene is still sitting up. "Thanks for talking me down from that freakout."

"Of course. Hey, before you pass out... What's up with Jake? I mean, I've seen PTSD before, like I said, but—there's a red flag I can barely make out. I don't know what it is."

"Jake may not have been on the front lines, but..." Carlos holds up his disfigured hand. "Everyone has different wounds. Everyone recovers differently. I can see who he is. Which is complicated, though."

"Why?"

"Gabi," Carlos sighs.

"Oh, fuck. Here we go!"

"No, it's not OK! I have to squash this."

"I'm rooting for you."

"Don't fucking tell anyone," Carlos pleads.

"I won't. The mushroom freakout story will do just fine," Gene says as they laugh.

Carlos's eyes slowly close and he falls into a deep sleep, his face warmed by the firelight while Gene turns his face up toward the cool white moon and stars.

12

THE TERRIBLE FLASHBACK

GENE AND MICHELLE WALK TOWARD THEIR HIGH SCHOOL'S amphitheater stage. The sun is already high in the sky for Day on the Green. They got out of class early to set up for their lunchtime performance. The stage sits in the middle of the school, a focal point in an open grass field where students hang out during lunch when there are no events or announcements.

Once every few months, the school allows students to perform during an extended lunch period called Day on the Green, featuring musical acts and other performances. This is the third time Gene and Michelle have auditioned—Gene singing and Michelle playing her acoustic guitar—and they finally got booked. The pair mostly do covers and a few originals. Even at this age, Michelle is a solid songwriter. Gene, however, just wants to be the star. He's not interested in composing. Sometimes Michelle convinces him to play a second guitar part she wrote, but it takes a lot of practice and persuading.

They finish the nerve-wracking task of plugging in cords and searching for power outlets, ensuring everything turns on. The student leading Day on the Green this year is a senior and the student body Activity Coordinator. He has a sharp, no-nonsense demeanor, his clipboard clutched tightly in one hand as he surveys the preparations. He approaches Gene with impatience-laced disdain. His gaze sweeps over Gene's unconventional attire: a Descendents t-shirt, ripped jeans, and thin, bleached dreadlocks. The rainbow pin on his shirt and his brown skin don't escape the coordinator's notice, either.

With an exaggerated sigh, he hands Gene the microphone. "Here. The comic hasn't arrived yet, so try not to break it," he mutters, his eyes narrowing as he scrutinizes Gene up and down.

Gene catches the look and the subtle sneer. He can't help but laugh, and he feels a sense of satisfaction as the coordinator shifts uncomfortably, clearly unsettled by the unspoken challenge.

"What's so funny?" the coordinator snaps. His fingers tighten around the clipboard until they turn white.

Gene grins, still chuckling. "Just you, man. Lighten up. It's a school event, not a corporate board meeting."

The coordinator's cheeks flush slightly, and he adjusts his grip on the clipboard. "Just don't break it, OK?"

Gene salutes mockingly. "Aye, aye, Captain." He turns away, still laughing, and walks toward the front of the stage, feeling a mixture of amusement and triumph.

Gene tests the mic. "Yellowww," he says. It works, no feedback. "OK, awesome," he says with relief. Michelle doesn't hear him; she's already playing her guitar, adjusting the EQ and volume knobs on her little combo amp to better fit the openness of the amphitheater. The sound bounces differently than in her carpeted bedroom with its low ceiling.

Students start to fill the grass area and take their seats up front as the bell rings. "What did you guys do? Ditch class to get that food already?" Gene asks into the mic at the kids in the front row.

"Shut up, asshole!" one yells back. Gene laughs as he puts the mic on the stand. Michelle mutes her guitar and leaves it on a stand by her amp. They walk behind the stage and hang out while a student attempts stand-up comedy to open the performances.

The grass area is now filled with students eating their lunches next to their backpacks, with dozens more watching while passing by on their way to other destinations.

"That guy's such an asshole," Gene tells Michelle, his eyes narrowing as he watches the student coordinator lord over the stage from the side.

"OK, I've decided," she says, staying focused on her task. "Set number 2."

"Alright," Gene says, disappointed. He turns back to Michelle, reassured by her quiet confidence. "'Dark Jam' and 'Living Room Jam' are great songs, though."

"Thanks. I just think more covers is best today. This is about getting them to sing along. They don't know our shit."

"This guy make you nervous? Jeez, no one's laughing. Poor guy."

The comic on stage stumbles through another joke, his voice wavering as the silence stretches on, amplifying the awkwardness.

"He's alright." Michelle's face goes blank, her focus intensifying. Gene catches the subtle shift in her expression, the way her eyes harden a bit too much, like she's putting on armor.

The comic tries to salvage his set with one last punchline, but it falls flat, leaving only a smattering of polite applause.

"Gene, Michelle, you're up," the coordinator calls out.

Gene and Michelle exchange nods, a silent acknowledgment of the task ahead. They stride back onto the stage with masked confidence. Gene takes the mic from the comic, sharing a quick high-five. Michelle retrieves her guitar from the stand, unmuting her amp with a practiced motion. They plunge into their first song before the applause dies.

Gene starts the verse, but horror strikes as the mic shocks him. He jerks his head back, almost dropping it. The coordinator winces.

Gene quickly regains his composure, but no sound comes from the PA system. He taps the mic, but it remains silent. He turns to Michelle, who keeps playing without missing a beat; she nods at him, signaling to keep going.

Gene drops the mic and walks to the edge of the stage. Leaning into the crowd, he belts out the song louder than ever before. His voice carries across the amphitheater. The crowd, impressed, begin to sing along, their voices merging with his impromptu chorus.

13

THE HORRIBLE CAMERA

GABI ADJUSTS HER CAMERA, FOCUSING ON JAKE, WHO STANDS alone on the stage in the musty basement of Gerry's. The lights set up for the photoshoot overpower the labored yellow bulbs attached to the ceiling, creating distinct contrasts and highlighting the rawness of the space. She snaps a few shots, capturing the focused expression on Jake's face.

"Hold still, Jake. Just a few more," she says, her voice soft but steady.

It's late morning, and upstairs, the restaurant is eerily quiet except for the muffled laughter and conversation of the rest of the band waiting their turn. Their voices drift down the staircase, creating a sense of anticipation.

Gabi takes another shot, adjusting her focus to capture the band's gear behind Jake. She shifts the lens, bringing into view the haphazard array of cables, amps, and the well-worn instruments scattered around the stage. Carlos's drum set, with its scuffed skins and faded logo, sits prominently in the background, a silent testament to countless hours of practice and performance.

"By Saturday, huh?" Gabi asks, her tone hopeful yet measured. "Ambitious."

"Oh yeah, totally. It hasn't been that hard," Jake replies, his eyes darting to the clutter of cables and equipment around them. "Tara's gear is so nice." Microphones are rigged to the amps and drums assembled on the stage behind him.

"Mixing sounds hard," Gabi says, peering into the viewfinder.

"Tara gave me some links to videos that have been helpful," Jake says, changing his pose. Gabi captures another shot, this time a close-up of his expression: a mix of determination and irritation. "I'm glad. Just annoyed that she made me responsible, though."

"How so?"

"It was my idea to record an EP ourselves," Jake starts. "She didn't have to patronize me by 'giving' the job to me."

Gabi's eyes flicker with understanding as she lowers her camera. "She just wants everything to go smoothly."

"Whatever. I'm gonna make it sound great."

Gabi nods, her focus shifting back to her camera. She captures a candid shot of Jake jumping down from the stage and smiles.

"Carlos! You're up!" Jake shouts.

Carlos walks down the stairs, watching Jake's session wrap up. A mix of nerves and excitement churns in his stomach. Jake gives him a high-five as he heads upstairs, and Carlos steps into the makeshift spotlight.

Gabi greets him with a smile, adjusting the lens. "Ready?"

Carlos nods, trying to ease his body.

"How's the recording going?" she asks, snapping a quick photo.

"Good, I think." Carlos shrugs, a grin tugging at his lips. "Most of the recording is done. Jake just has to mix it now."

Gabi directs his poses, her voice calm and soothing. "Try to relax. Why are you so tense?"

"The attention on just me makes me uncomfortable," Carlos admits, his expression betraying his unease.

Gabi captures the internal struggle on his face, the flash illuminating his discomfort. She lowers the camera slightly. "It's just me, Carlos. Pretend we're back at Best Buy, talking about lenses."

Carlos chuckles softly, his shoulders loosening a bit.

Gabi smiles, her eyes never leaving his. "So, Carlos, why do you love music?" she asks, her tone gentle but probing.

"Oh, god. You and your questions," he laughs. "Music makes me focus on the present. I'm so concentrated on not messing up that I don't think about much else."

"Oh, come on. Be honest with me."

Carlos lowers his shoulders, forgetting his pose. "It makes me so happy. Like I'm doing something that is pure joy. Especially with other people. These guys are like my family. I want them to be my family."

"So it's not as satisfying by yourself?"

"It's just better with someone else."

"So, drumming by yourself is like masturbating, and collaboration is sex."

"Exactly," Carlos says, blushing. Gabi captures the moment, her camera clicking as she catches the raw vulnerability in his eyes. She snaps a few more photos, adjusting her angle. "Tilt your head slightly to the left," she directs, her voice soft but firm.

Carlos breathes deeply, feeling a sense of calm wash over him. Gabi's presence, her humor, and the way she sees him make it easier to let go. He shoots her a warm smile, his eyes sparkling with a hint of mischief. "Is this my good side?" he teases.

Gabi chuckles, lowering her camera for a moment. "Every

side is your good side," she quips back, her own smile widening as she raises the camera again. "Now, look off into the distance like you're in a serious band," she chuckles.

Carlos follows her direction, his thoughts drifting but anchored by her laughter and the warmth in her gaze. Gabi's attention feels like sunlight, brightening the shadows of his mind. He glances back at her, his smile deepening.

"You're a natural, Carlos," she says, lowering the camera and meeting his eyes. "Maybe I should hire you as my muse."

Carlos chuckles. "I'd be honored," he replies, his voice carrying a note of flirtation. "As long as I get to see more of your work."

Gabi's eyes twinkle. "Deal," she says, and for a moment, the world narrows to just the two of them, sharing a connection through the lens and the unspoken words between them.

"What are you two doing down there?" Jake calls out as he descends the stairs. His eyes flick to Carlos, then settle on Gabi with a smile. "Ready for the group photo now, or what?"

"Yeah, we just wrapped," Gabi says, trying to hide her flushed cheeks. She adjusts her camera, focusing on the settings to avoid meeting Jake's gaze.

"Group photo time!" Jake yells up the stairs. He strides over, plants a quick kiss on Gabi's lips, then stands beside Carlos, draping an arm around him. Carlos stiffens, but forces a grin.

"OK, everyone, gather up," Gabi says.

Gene and Michelle shuffle down the stairs, taking their positions next to Carlos and Jake. Seeing Jake's arm around Carlos, they follow suit, forming a line locked together. Gabi raises her camera, snapping a few shots and checking the composition.

"Alright, hold that pose, guys," she directs, her voice steady. "Just checking the settings."

Jake's arm tightens slightly around Carlos. "You sure we look good?" he asks, glancing at Gabi, his tone tight.

Gabi nods, focusing on her camera. "You look great. Michelle, tilt your head a bit. Gene, move in closer."

The band adjusts as instructed, and Gabi captures the moment.

The artists' entrance door at the back swings open, and Tara walks in holding a plastic to-go bag. "Hey guys, I've got some news coming," she announces. "As soon as the EP is done, Jake, let me know. I need a copy as soon as possible."

"I'll finish the mix today. But I'll need a day to export it onto CDs and write our name on them. It should be ready by Saturday for the show," Jake says, looking proud. The rest of the band share an excited smile at the plan.

"Send me 'Cloneville' first before you do anything else. I need one song to send out."

Jake nods.

Tara gives them a quick smile, places the to-go bag next to the door, then leaves, closing it behind her.

"OK," Gene laughs.

Michelle walks over to inspect the bag. "Tacos!"

"Alright, let's get these group shots done already," commands Gabi sharply. Michelle returns to the group and they gather for the last shot.

"Smile and say EP!" Gene shouts.

14

THE TERRIBLE CIGARETTE

SATURDAY NIGHT AT GERRY'S, THE BAND TAKES THE STAGE FOR the show. Tara's promise of news is still ringing in Carlos's ears. The basement is packed, the crowd alive and filling every inch of space. The air is thick with anticipation, but Carlos's focus narrows to the drum kit in front of him. As he settles in, his hands steady with his sticks, the familiar surge of adrenaline kicks in. The noise of the crowd fades, replaced by the steady thump of his heartbeat. This is where everything else falls away —the only place where his mind feels clear. He takes a deep breath and clicks his sticks together for the count-in. The first beat is like a pulse, grounding him, the rhythm pulling him into a world where nothing else matters.

The band now has a synergy that can only come from hours of practice and a deep connection. Their passion is contagious, and each member plays and sings without mistakes—except when Jake, caught up in his performance and his lust for the spotlight, forgets to sing his backup parts. Michelle glances at him, her eyes narrowing in quiet disapproval, but she keeps playing.

The audience is enthralled, their energy feeding back to the

band. Faces in the crowd mirror Carlos's intensity, eyes wide
and unblinking, bodies moving in sync with the pounding
rhythm. Sweat glistens on their foreheads, a testament to their
shared exertion.

Carlos loses himself in the rhythm, the beats of his drums
matching the pulse of the room. He can see heads bobbing,
arms pumping, and feet stomping, all in perfect time with his
drumming. It's as if the entire room breathes in unison with
each strike of the drumstick, creating a symphony of collective
heartbeats and breath.

An invisible thread weaves through the crowd and back to
Carlos, amplifying his energy and driving him to hit harder,
play faster. He's in the zone, every beat perfectly timed, every
movement fluid and precise. The basement is alive, and for a
moment, the music and the crowd are one, a single, unified
force riding the waves of sound.

TARA SPILLS the news out front with some fresh air after the set.
The cool air bites at Carlos's damp skin, a reminder that winter
is approaching. "Well, first off, Jake, your EP sold out. So
excellent idea recording it ourselves," she starts. "Second, I got
the Elden Aldo Show people to come watch. They were in the
crowd."

"What?" they all yell in unison.

"Yup, here they are now." Tara points to two older men
walking out of Gerry's wearing polos and jeans. "I got in contact
with them through one of my YouTube subscribers who works
for the network. When I brought up the band, they agreed to
drive up from L.A. to see you guys perform."

Carlos feels his heart pounding. The Elden Aldo Show is
huge. He exchanges a look with Jake, who is visibly stunned.
Carlos can hardly believe what's happening. As the show's
representatives step forward, the band members straighten up,

trying to maintain their cool. Tara introduces them to the band, and the reality of the moment sinks in.

"Hey," one of the representatives says with a friendly smile, extending a hand. "You guys were incredible tonight. We'd love to talk more about having you on the show."

As they stand side by side, Jake eagerly bumps Carlos's hand out of the way to shake the representative's hand first. His eyes gleam with self-importance, as if he's already envisioning "his" band's future success. Carlos feels a pang of irritation at the subtle snub and Jake's lack of awareness.

The representative continues to smile, seemingly oblivious to the tension, and says, "I really think you guys have something special."

They book it. The representatives leave with Tara and the band jumps up and down in a celebratory group hug. Carlos peeks over his shoulder and notices Houston standing by the front door smoking a cigarette. Breaking free of the group hug, he walks over.

"Hey!" Carlos yells.

"Carlos! What's up, dude?" Houston shouts back. "Nice playing. You guys killed it."

"Thanks! Glad you were able to make it," Carlos says, still out of breath from the news.

"Your lead guitar player was going nuts," Houston says, dropping his cigarette and grinding it into the ground.

"Right?" Carlos laughs. "And we just got booked for the Elden Aldo Show next month! Like, it *just* happened!"

"Dude! Congrats. Looks like a good direction. Pretty soon you're gonna have to quit Best Buy," Houston mutters, eyes cast downward. "Rather than calling in sick all the time... I'm rooting for you." Carlos, basking in his triumph, misses the tightness in Houston's tone.

"Thanks, man, I really appreciate that. Wouldn't have happened if you hadn't hooked me up with that interview."

"Well, speaking of," Houston starts, forcing a smile, "I'm the new assistant manager. Promotion! Woot!"

"That's fantastic! Look at you."

"Right? Doing alright, if I do say so myself," Houston says, adjusting an invisible tie. "So, I'm assuming you'll need to request more time off..." He drops his arms. Just as it looks like he's about to say more, he grabs Carlos's shoulder, a bit harder than necessary. "Keep killing it, man. See you at work." Houston turns away before Carlos can respond. He nearly bumps shoulders with Michelle as she appears from the front door.

"Carlos, you coming?" she says from the threshold. "We still have to pack up." He nods and gives her a thumbs-up. As he watches Michelle disappear back inside, his gut tightens, and his eyebrows furrow. He rubs his shoulder where Houston's hand had pressed down. Shaking his head to dispel the confusion, Carlos heads back inside, his steps heavier than before.

15

THE HORRIBLE SPOTLIGHT

"... AND YOU FELL OFF THE STAGE!" GENE LAUGHS, HIS VOICE carrying a mix of nostalgia and amusement. The group drives through the yellow valleys between the snowy hills of the Grapevine on their way to L.A. for the Elden Aldo Show. Reminiscing about one of his and Michelle's first performances in high school distracts the group from their nerves about the impending performance.

"Yeah, I thought I was going to die of embarrassment," Michelle chimes in, her voice still tinged with the youthful exuberance of that high school performance. "Surprised I didn't break anything."

Carlos looks over at Jake, who's fast asleep with his head leaning against the window, the shape of his breath slowly condensing on the cold glass. He feels a pang of envy. Michelle and Gene have so many shared memories, a history he's only recently become a part of. Tara and Gabi plan on meeting the band at the studio, and without them here he feels even more alone. He taps out a beat on his lap. The rhythm soothes him, a small reminder of the control he can exert over his nerves.

They wind along in their newly acquired van, a symbol of

their growing success—despite the faint wet-dog smell masked by cedar air fresheners. It's an older model but reliable, one that Tara's dad gave them a deal on from one of his many dealerships across California.

Carlos gazes out the window. The undeveloped space between the two cities, with its winding roads and stunning ridges hinting at snow this time of year, offers a brief respite from their anxiety. The snow-dusted hills are a striking contrast to the Iraqi desert, he reminisces. He remembers how flat it was. And how bright the sand was.

Michelle, who's driving, swerves to avoid a piece of debris in the road.

Just like that, Carlos is back in Iraq, driving a fuel truck through a desolate landscape. The heat is oppressive, and the constant threat of IEDs keeps him on edge despite the cheerful music playing on his iPod. He remembers the explosion that changed everything, the percussion that felt like every inch of his body being punched at the same time. His music miraculously continued playing, injecting a shred of eeriness into the chaos.

"Hey, Carlos." Gene's voice pulls him back to the present. "When you clap, is it weird?"

"No," he laughs, shoving his scarred hand in Gene's face.

"Don't make me take your thumb," Gene jokes. They continue down the Grapevine, the anticipation of their performance fueling their conversation and turning their nervous energy into hopeful excitement.

UPON ARRIVING AT THE STUDIO, they are greeted by Gabi, Tara, and a production assistant, who leads them through a maze of corridors to hair and make-up. The walls are lined with photos of famous performers who have graced the stage before them.

After their brief, Carlos, Michelle, and Gene huddle around

Michelle's iPod, playing their favorite tracks to pump themselves up for the performance. Jake, however, paces the room, eating the Sour Patch Kids left for the band on the coffee table in the middle of the room.

Michelle takes out her guitar and begins teaching Carlos a guitar part she wrote. It's a catchy riff that Jake usually plays, but she wants to show Carlos how it's done to pass the time. Jake overhears and can't resist making a snide comment. "Look at you, trying to be a guitar player now." Carlos laughs it off, but it's a tense laugh rather than an easygoing one.

The same production assistant swings open the door. "The Horrible Terribles, you're up."

As they step onto the stage, the lights are blinding, casting a brilliant glow that makes the entire set shimmer. The audience's murmurs blend into a distant hum, a low vibration of excitement and anticipation. The set features a sleek, modern design with a large, illuminated backdrop displaying the show's iconic logo.

With a nod from a crew member, the band launches into their most popular song, the song they usually use to close their local sets. With electrifying energy and precision, each note resonates through the state-of-the-art sound system. The crowd, curious at first, quickly catches on to the infectious melody, heads nodding in sync with the driving beat.

Elden Aldo, the host whose name is synonymous with late-night television, watches from the sidelines. She is a towering figure in the entertainment world, known for her charisma and sharp wit. Her presence commands attention, her every gesture exuding confidence and importance. As the song concludes, she strides onto the stage with the ease of a seasoned performer.

The audience erupts into applause, and Elden, with her signature smile, approaches the band. She shakes hands with Gene, her grip firm and her eyes sparkling with genuine admiration. "Great job, Gene! Your voice is incredible," she says, her voice warm and full of praise. The cameras capture every moment, broadcasting her approval to millions of viewers.

Jake stands nearby, his expression carefully controlled. Carlos can sense the anger simmering beneath the surface, even though Jake is trying to keep his cool. He knows Jake well enough to understand the sting of being overlooked he must be feeling, but Jake isn't about to release that anger on television.

Elden turns to the audience, her smile never faltering. "Wasn't that just amazing?" she exclaims, eliciting another wave of applause. "Stay tuned, because we have even more incredible performances coming up next!" She winks at the camera, and the show cuts to a commercial break. The studio hums with energy and the band basks in the afterglow of their performance.

As THEY RETURN to the green room, the band is still buzzing with the high of their performance, but Carlos sees Jake's forced smile and the disappointment in his eyes. He knows exactly what's bothering him. "Dude, she totally ignored me too, but I'm not mad. Gene's the singer, it happens."

"Fuck you, Carlos. You people pleaser," Jake snaps, his frustration spilling over.

Carlos flinches at the harsh words but tries to stay calm. "Jake, come on, man. We're a band. We're in this together." The energy in the room shifts as Jake's anger lingers in the air, a silent threat to their unity.

"Exactly. A band. What am I? The hired hand?"

"You guys, chill," Michelle jumps in.

Carlos feels the weight of the situation pressing on him. The band has been his escape, his solace from the chaos of his mind. But now, it feels like the very thing that keeps him grounded might be slipping away. He glances around, noticing the uneasy glances between Gene and Michelle.

Before the tension can escalate further, Tara and Gabi burst in, barely able to contain their excitement. Gabi runs up and hugs Jake. "Guys, you were amazing! And guess what? Dangerous Penguin Records wants to sign you!"

"They saw the performance and loved it!" Tara adds. The room erupts in cheers, the echoes bouncing off the walls like the aftermath of an earthquake. Carlos feels a surge of relief wash over him as he looks around, seeing the joy on his bandmates' faces. Even Jake seems to forget his attitude for a moment, joining in the celebration with a deep, genuine smile.

Back in Bakersfield, word of their successful performance spreads like wildfire. Fans flood their social media with congratulatory messages, each notification adding to the band's growing sense of accomplishment. Local press outlets clamor for interviews, eager to feature the rising stars in their columns.

The band rides this wave of excitement. Yet, amid the celebration, Jake's bitterness festers. Carlos notices the tension in Jake's shoulders whenever he scrolls through the comments when they ignore him, and the way his smile doesn't quite reach his eyes during interviews.

16

THE TERRIBLE BUILD-UP

"WHAT HAPPENED TO YOUR ROOM?" GABI ASKS AS SHE WALKS inside. Jake's room is filled with musical paraphernalia: a keyboard, a clarinet, a marimba, a harmonium, an old wooden toy piano, and a mandolin. Each instrument is meticulously arranged, reflecting Jake's pride and excitement. Printed music tabs are spread out everywhere, adding to the sense of creative chaos.

"I added to my collection."

"I don't understand." Gabi squints her eyes.

"Borrowed, rented, saved money, you know. Now I have a collection," Jake says, waving his arm around the room. "I haven't seen you as much lately outside the band."

Gabi's eyes widen with genuine admiration as she takes in the scene. "Wow, you've been busy."

Jake grins, picking up the clarinet. "Check this out." He plays the opening melody to "Grand Theft Autumn" by Fall Out Boy—her favorite song—the notes floating smoothly through the room.

"Aww, you learned that? Was that the first song you learned?" she asks, smiling.

"No," Jake laughs. "The first was the beginning of 'God Only Knows' by the Beach Boys."

"Oh," Gabi says, nodding. "That's impressive."

He sets the clarinet down and points to the array of instruments. "I'm gonna try and play a different instrument on every song on this new album, like Brian Jones did on the Stones' record *Aftermath*."

"That's awesome."

"I think this is gonna be an outstanding album. Hopefully, now I can have some spotlight."

Gabi's smile fades. "Is that really why you're doing this?"

"Most of why, yeah. Why? What's wrong with that?"

"It's Elden Aldo all over again. Why are you so concerned with being the face of this?"

"Gabi, I started this fucking band." Jake thumps his hand against his chest. "I named it, found the members, secured the rehearsal space, even fucking styled the band, recorded our EP, and what?" He throws open his arms and gestures wildly around the room. "*Gene* gets all the attention? He only sings! And barely at that!"

"He plays bass, too."

"OK, fine. Bass and sings."

"You're different now," she says, her voice barely above a whisper.

"I'm just being honest!" Jake retorts.

Gabi shakes her head, frustration bubbling up. "I need some air." She leaves the room before she gets too upset, leaving Jake standing among his instruments, confusion etched on his face. He sighs and picks up the clarinet again, playing aimlessly to fill the silence.

ABOUT AN HOUR LATER, Gabi returns with Tara following close behind. The two of them head straight inside, a sense of purpose in their strides. Jake doesn't look up as they enter, too absorbed in the melodic tune he's weaving.

"Jake," Tara calls, her voice cutting through the music. "We need to talk."

He lowers the clarinet, a frown creasing his forehead. "About what?"

"Your attitude. It's been shitty."

"I'm OK," he says, avoiding her eyes.

"Why was Gabi outside then?"

"Our relationship's not in your jurisdiction."

"She's talking about the band, Jake." Gabi sighs.

Jake's eyes flash with frustration. "Why am I the asshole here?"

"You *are* being an asshole." Gabi is losing her cool.

"Hey, both of you, calm down. This isn't helping." Tara steps between them, raising her hands to keep the peace. "No one's against you, Jake," she says, her voice firm. "But we can't keep going like this. We need to find a way to work together."

"We all want this band to succeed. Can you try to see it from our perspective?" Gabi asks.

"Which is?"

"Which is that there's one member of the band pulling his weight in the wrong direction," Tara reveals.

He nods, distracted. "Fine. I need to practice now."

"Good. That's a start." Tara gives him a reassuring pat on the shoulder as she notices the musical build-up. "What is all this, anyway?"

"Gonna try and play different instruments on the album."

"Like Brian Jones," Gabi explains with a sigh.

"Does Michelle know?"

"They'll be stoked," Jake reassures her.

Tara walks back outside with Gabi, leaving Jake alone once more. He picks up his clarinet again, but this time the notes are erratic, frustrated.

17

THE HORRIBLE OBSESSION

CARLOS, MICHELLE, AND GENE ARRIVE AT THE RECORDING studio, a dark wooden building tucked among a row of ordinary businesses on a busy L.A. street. There's no sign, and they can barely see it over a solid black metal gate. Carlos squints at the MapQuest printout in his hand.

"This is it?" he asks, holding the paper up to the afternoon sun.

Gene nods, peering through an opening. "Not as glamorous as I imagined."

Carlos chuckles.

Michelle pushes open the gate and they step into the small courtyard, glancing around at the modest surroundings. A red Toyota Prius appears to be using the courtyard as a parking lot. The building itself seems almost forgotten, but there's a certain charm in its simplicity.

The producer opens the door, offering a pleasant smile. "Hey, guys! Welcome. Reuben from the emails," he introduces himself. He has a long brown beard and a slight belly, with warm eyes that twinkle beneath his short hair. He's wearing jeans, a black pullover sweater, and Adidas slides with white socks. "I just got off the phone with Gabi. They'll be here in a few minutes," he says, ushering them inside.

Gabi is representing the band for this first session—her idea—and Jake had jumped at the chance to ride with her rather than with his bandmates. Carlos thought back to Jake's overeager expression with a sense of unease.

Carlos steps into the studio, taking in the polished wood and glass, and the state-of-the-art equipment gleaming under the warm, comforting lamps. There are two rooms separated by a large window. The room they're in has a fluffy, worn-out couch a few feet away, facing a large mixing board. Behind the glass is an open space with different style rugs collaging the floor. The space radiates a quiet energy, a promise of creativity waiting to be unleashed.

"Whoa," Michelle says, looking through the glass.

Carlos runs his fingers over the mixing board, feeling the smooth, cool surface. "This place is amazing," he says, his voice barely audible.

"Go ahead and start setting up while we wait for the others," Reuben instructs.

In the room behind the glass, Carlos sets up his drums meticulously, tuning each one to perfection. He adjusts the cymbals, checks the stands and pedals, and tests the sound. It isn't until long after everyone else has already warmed up that the room finally fills with the rich, resonant tones of his drums, blending with the ambient noise of the wooden studio.

Minutes later, Jake and Gabi arrive. Jake immediately dives into setting up his guitar and amp, his movements precise but frantic, somehow—a stark contrast to Carlos's measured approach.

Carlos feels a flutter in his chest when he catches Gabi's eye as she moves to talk with Reuben. She gives Carlos an encouraging smile. He feels a mix of excitement and nervousness—and a sudden self-consciousness about his appearance. Quickly glancing at his reflection in the glass divider, he runs his scarred hand through his growing curls and adjusts the flat spot from his nap in the van.

Gabi sits on a chair at the edge of the room, camera now in hand. She stays out of the way, snapping photos of the band, always ready in case she's needed.

Reuben, whose calm demeanor exudes the expertise of a seasoned professional, gathers the band and takes charge of the pre-production process. "Today is a crucial day as we begin to rehearse together in order to dial in all your parts before we hit record," he explains. "Jake, I understand you brought a bunch of instruments. We'll talk about that too."

"They're still in the trunk." Jake springs up, eager to show off his collection. "I'll go get them."

"In a minute." Reuben waves him back down. "Let's first focus on the songs with two guitars before we experiment. It's nice out, they'll be fine."

Jake's face tightens. He slumps back into his seat, his foot tapping impatiently. Carlos notices the disappointment radiating from his friend, but Reuben's calm, patient approach eases his own nerves.

They exchange a few words about expectations and schedules, Reuben's steady voice cutting through the underlying excitement in the room. With a nod from Reuben, they jump into their first song.

DURING A BREAK, Carlos notices Michelle sitting on the worn-out couch, strumming her guitar quietly. He walks over and sits beside her.

"Hey, you OK?" he asks, his voice gentle.

Michelle sighs, her fingers still moving over the strings. "Yeah, just... today has been great, focusing on our guitars. I like having two guitar parts, you know?"

Carlos nods, then asks, "Do you feel like your songs aren't gonna come out the way you wrote them? Or is it just different without two?"

"Both, honestly," Michelle replies. "My parts feel incomplete, and the songs sound different now."

"Have you talked to Reuben about it?" Carlos asks, genuinely concerned.

"Not yet. I don't want to mess with what's working. Besides, I can't deny they sound great at Gerry's. Big picture thinking, I guess."

Carlos gives her a reassuring smile. "We wouldn't sound the same without you."

Michelle offers a small grin.

The front door opens, letting in a cool breeze and a bright light as Gabi returns with Reuben. Gene and Jake look up from their conversation in the open room.

"OK, let's get back to it," Reuben says. "We'll have to get to your songs next time, Jake." Jake stares for a moment, then smiles, but his shoulders drop. He slings his guitar over his shoulder and unmutes it, playing with the feedback. Carlos and Michelle return to their instruments as well. They play their first song over and over again.

Carlos feels a surge of optimism. He soaks in every piece of advice Reuben gives on their performance, eager to learn and improve. He looks over and notices Jake's intensity growing. His playing becomes more aggressive, almost desperate to stand out.

"Try loosening up a bit, Jake," Reuben suggests. Jake's eyes narrow slightly. Reuben doesn't notice as he turns to Gene. "Gene, nice job not losing the bass line while singing that chorus." Jake's fingers twitch on the fretboard, his jaw set.

18

THE TERRIBLE CAT

JAKE SITS AT THE DIM BAR UPSTAIRS AT GERRY'S, NURSING A drink. There's no music tonight, so the room is filled with the soft hum of conversations and the occasional clink of glasses. The worn wooden counter in front of him feels like a familiar friend, bearing the weight of his frustrations.

"I've failed at everything, Gerry," Jake says, his voice tinged with defeat.

Gerry wipes the counter with a practiced hand, his expression calm. "You don't know what failure is," he replies, rolling his eyes. "You're still young, Jake. You've got plenty of time to figure shit out."

Jake sighs, staring into his drink. "I was captain of my soccer team, you know. Could've gone pro. Then the whole 'Join the army! Fight for your country! Be the hero we always see in World War II movies!' What a load of shit," he says, slamming his glass against the counter. "There was only bullshit over there. Now music. I can't even get that right."

"Oh, shut up," Gerry chuckles softly, shaking his head. "You're too hard on yourself. You know, everyone's got their own path. It's not always about the big, flashy victories."

Jake looks up, his eyes dull. "But what if my path is just a dead end again? What if I never amount to anything?"

Gerry leans on the counter, meeting Jake's gaze. "Your little EP there is selling great. You're making me some money now," he says, playful yet serious. "Don't be so concerned with glory, kid. Life isn't just about the big moments. It's about the small ones, too. The connections you make, the lives you touch. You've got a gift, even if you can't see it right now."

Jake feels a wave of nausea, his stomach churning. He glances at the nearly empty glass in front of him. "I think I need to head home," he manages to say, pushing his stool back and standing up unsteadily.

Gerry eyes him with concern. "You look like shit. Go home, get some rest. And remember, you're not alone in this. We all have our battles."

Jake nods. "Thanks, Gerry."

"Wait, you're not driving, are you?"

"No," Jake slurs.

Gerry picks up the bar phone and starts to dial.

"I'm walking, I swear!" Jake shouts. Gerry hangs up the phone and squints his eyes.

Jake musters a smile and heads toward the stairs, descending to the basement. The air grows cooler as he steps down. He pauses at the bottom. His gaze sweeps across the empty stage, its worn wooden floor spray-painted black, and the scattered cables hinting at recent activity. The faint scent of stale beer and body odor lingers in the air. After a moment, he walks with purpose to the artists' entrance door, his footsteps echoing in the quiet space.

Outside, in the alley, the warm night air envelops him. Jake stands for a moment, feeling the heat of the day still radiating from the walls. He breathes deeply, the dry air filling his lungs. The narrow alley is lined with old, brick walls, their rough texture visible in the glow of a nearby streetlight.

Trash cans are haphazardly placed along the walls, their lids slightly askew. Jake's breath comes slow and steady as he exhales, his hands resting at his sides. He takes another deep breath, the air thick and warm, and notices a white cat with orange blotches darting across the alley. Its sleek body weaves between the trash cans. He watches it for a moment, then stretches, his muscles tense from the evening.

Suddenly, he feels a tug at his back pocket. He spins around, coming face to face with a man with ragged brown teeth visible through a crooked smile and a worn green field jacket hanging loosely on his thin frame—the same man who robbed him before. The man yanks Jake's phone from his pocket with a swift, practiced motion, then bolts down the alley, legs pumping furiously, jacket flapping behind him like a cape.

"Fuck this," Jake mutters, adrenaline kicking in. He bolts after the man, feet pounding the pavement. A cop, noticing the commotion, joins the chase from down the street. Jake's lungs burn, but he pushes on, gaining on the mugger. With a final burst of speed, he tackles the man to the ground. They grapple, rolling on the gritty asphalt. Just as Jake is about to land a punch, the cop's shout distracts him.

"Stop right there!"

The mugger seizes the distraction, shoving Jake off balance. He pulls a knife, the blade catching the light as it flashes between them. They grapple for control, bodies slamming into the ground, the gritty pavement scraping against their skin. Legs tangled, arms straining, they roll and twist, each fighting for dominance. The cop now sprints toward them, his footsteps pounding in the distance.

Jake's fingers slip over the knife handle, slick with sweat. He struggles to wrestle it loose, his muscles burning with the effort. Finally, the knife falls to the ground with a sharp clatter. The mugger lunges, fingertips grazing the blade, but Jake kicks it away, sending it skidding across the asphalt, just out of reach.

In a swift, brutal move, the mugger punches Jake, knocking him flat on his back. Free from Jake's grip, he scrambles to grab the knife. Kneeling over Jake, the mugger raises the blade high, eyes glinting with menace. Time seems to slow as the knife starts to descend.

A loud bang shatters the air. The mugger's body jolts, then collapses to the side. The knife slips from his hand, clattering harmlessly beside them. Jake scrambles to his feet, noticing the blood spreading from the mugger's arm.

"Ah, damn it," the mugger groans in agony from the ground.

Jake grabs his phone from the asphalt with trembling hands. "I'm sorry," he mumbles to the cop, voice barely audible over the pounding in his ears.

The mugger winces, looking up at Jake with a mix of pain and anger.

"You'll have to come with me," the cop calls after him, stepping forward and reaching out. Jake hesitates for a split second, seeing the cop's serious expression and the radio crackling with calls for backup.

Without another word, Jake bolts up the alley. The cop shouts after him but quickly turns his attention back to the bleeding mugger. Jake keeps running, his heart racing and breath coming in short, ragged gasps.

He weaves through the trash and debris, driven by a primal urge to escape. The distant sound of sirens sends a jolt through his body, but the cop's voice fades as he turns the corner, putting more distance between them.

19

THE HORRIBLE FUTURE

CARLOS AND GABI STROLL THROUGH THE BAKERSFIELD COLLEGE art gallery, their footsteps echoing softly against the concrete floors. The space is adorned with a variety of artworks, from vibrant abstract paintings to intricate sculptures, each piece telling its own story. Simple track lighting highlights the pieces, casting subtle shadows that bring the textures to life.

As they walk, Carlos notices that Gabi's usual enthusiasm for art seems dampened. Her eyes, which normally sparkle with excitement, are clouded with worry, and her steps are slower, more deliberate. Her shoulders are slightly hunched, and she fiddles absentmindedly with the strap of her bag.

"What's wrong?" he asks, breaking the silence.

Gabi sighs, pausing in front of a large, melancholic painting, her gaze unfocused. It's a very minimal image—only two shades of gray against a dirty white background. There's an anguished figure crouching in the center made up of only three simple lines. "I'm worried about Jake. He used to be so open and warm. Even when he came back home from the war, he was his normal sweet self."

"Maybe I bring it out of him," Carlos suggests, trying to lighten the mood.

"No. How?" Gabi stares at him, puzzled.

"I felt a tinge of jealousy when we first talked about our deployments. Don't know what that means, but it seems like something," he admits.

"No, he really likes you. He's told me a bunch," she reassures him.

"Well, then I'm not gonna pretend to know." Carlos laughs, though his eyes betray a hint of concern.

"When we got back together, right before he left for the army, we told each other we would write every day. It was so romantic," Gabi reminisces, her voice softening.

"That is sweet," Carlos says, his voice steady, though something tightens in his chest.

"Yeah! I love that stuff. I get he's all-in for this band, but he's acting like his life depends on it." Her frustration is evident.

Carlos chuckles. "But recording is done now. Which he was awesome on. So I don't know what his deal is."

"I know! I'm so happy for you guys." Gabi forces a smile that doesn't reach her eyes.

Carlos grins and claps, but Gabi is no longer looking at the art; her thoughts are elsewhere, and her mood has clearly shifted. He realizes his mistake and steers the conversation back to her. "But anyway, you were looking at this painting."

Gabi's face brightens a bit as she begins to explain. "This piece here," she points to the melancholic painting, "is by another student, Evie Davis. She's graduating soon too. She's known for her use of minimal color and texture to convey emotion in her paintings, and her simple but critical photos."

Carlos listens intently, genuinely curious. "Do you know her personally?"

"Yeah, I met her in a class last year. She's really cool, always very honest," Gabi replies, her dark eyes brightening.

"Does her work inspire you?" Carlos looks from the painting back to her.

"Definitely. She taught me to experiment more with my photography, to take risks, to be more honest," Gabi explains.

"That's cool. Have you ever been in one of these shows before now?" Carlos inquires, his curiosity growing.

"No, this is my first time," she shakes her head. "It's such an honor to have my photo displayed here."

"That's amazing, Gabi. This is awesome," he says, his excitement palpable.

"Thanks," she says listlessly. "I was hoping Jake would be here to see it, but..."

"I'm sorry he's always busy now," Carlos manages after a short pause. Gabi continues down the hall of the gallery. "I'm glad you brought me. You did owe me art, though. Remember?" he calls out behind her. She turns and winks.

They continue their tour in silence, and as they turn a corner, Carlos notices a photograph that looks familiar. "Hey! That's us, right? One of yours?" He points to a striking black-and-white photo of the whole band sitting on a curb, eating burritos wrapped in foil. The image captures a casual, candid moment, with the band members absorbed in their meals, except for Jake, who sits front and center. He stares directly into the lens, his expression radiating happiness and warmth, while the others are focused on their food.

Gabi smiles, a genuine warmth in her eyes. "Yeah, it is! It's just called *Jake Robbins*. I was hoping this would show Jake that he's important to the band, to give him more confidence." The photo's composition draws the viewer's attention to Jake, emphasizing his central role and capturing the essence of the band's camaraderie. The contrast in the black-and-white tones highlights the textures of their surroundings, from the crinkled foil of the burritos to the rough pavement of the sidewalk, creating a striking, evocative image.

Carlos takes a step back, examining her work. Gabi steals a glance at his face, a smile forming as her palms begin to sweat.

"This is amazing, Gabi. I'm so proud of you. Your work really deserves to be here." Carlos finally takes his eyes off the photo to meet hers.

"Thanks. That means a lot to me."

"What are you gonna do after you're done here?"

Gabi hesitates, then confesses, "I've been applying for transfers. I want to go to New York City or London. My dream schools are there. But I don't think Jake can go with me. I don't know if I even want him to go with me."

Carlos can see the conflict in her face. "That's a big decision. But it sounds like an amazing opportunity."

"Yeah," Gabi says, a hint of sadness in her voice.

Carlos breaks the sudden silence. "I gave Houston my two weeks' notice. He said I can have my job back in case the band fails," he laughs. "I don't get that guy."

Gabi smiles genuinely this time. "That's good, I guess. It's always nice to have a backup plan."

20

THE TERRIBLE DECLINE

THE BAND GATHERS IN THEIR REHEARSAL SPACE IN GERRY'S basement. Gene sits with his back against Carlos's bass drum, scribbling in a black notebook, occasionally lifting his head. Michelle is seated on the edge of the stage, restringing her guitar. Her fingers move deftly, her eyes occasionally shifting to the door.

Carlos sits behind his drum kit, stretching. He holds his right arm against his chest, scanning the basement. His eyes stop at Jake's amp and the guitar case leaning against it. A bottle of anxiety pills with one left on top catches his attention. He remembers the early days when they were just friends with a shared dream. Now, with success within their grasp, holding this dream together feels like trying to catch smoke.

The sound of footsteps descending the stairs from the restaurant snaps Carlos back to the present. Gabi and Tara appear, each carrying a box. The room shares a collective sigh.

"Jake's still not here?" Gabi asks, glancing around as she sets her box down in front of the stage.

"Nope," Michelle says, tossing her old strings into the trash.

Tara sighs. "Well, here are more EPs. There was a mix-up

with shipping, so we just drove down and got them," she says, placing her box alongside Gabi's.

Carlos looks up from behind his cymbals. "Any news from Reuben?"

"We got an album release date," Gabi says, a hint of excitement in her voice. "September 1st. It's coming up, so we gotta talk tour."

"Sorry," a voice calls from the back of the basement. Jake stumbles in, glancing behind him before closing the artists' entrance door. He's sweating, with a faded black eye marking his face. His bloodshot, distant eyes avoid everyone's gaze. He heads straight to his guitar, not acknowledging anyone. The band members exchange quick glances before awkwardly returning to their instruments.

"Alright, let's go," Carlos says, tapping his drumsticks together, setting the tempo. Gene adjusts his bass strap, focused. Michelle takes a deep breath, her hand tight around the neck of her guitar.

Jake strums the opening chords, but the sound is flat, lacking its former vibrancy. The rest of the band joins in, playing with precision and professionalism. They manage to get through the song, but it's clear Jake is off.

Carlos reads the frustration on Michelle's face as she steps forward, her eyes fixed on Jake.

"Jake, you can't keep doing this," she groans as she places her guitar in a stand by her amp. "We need you here, focused."

Carlos exchanges a glance with Gene, who's tapping his foot impatiently. Michelle crosses her arms, her eyes narrowing.

Jake looks down, avoiding everyone's eyes. "I'm sorry, I just... I'm not feeling well today."

"Not feeling well?" Michelle snaps. "We're all tired, Jake, but we still show up. You have to pull your weight."

Jake's eyes dart around the room, restless. He zeroes in on

Gabi, who sits quietly, her hands folded in her lap. His gaze shifts over the others, finally landing on Michelle again. His fists clench at his sides, his nostrils flaring as he takes a deep breath.

Then he fixes his stare back on Gabi. She remains calm and composed, her eyes briefly meeting Jake's before flicking away. His face reddens, and he takes a step forward, his posture tense. Without a word, he leans his guitar against his amp, grabs his pill bottle, and walks out of the basement. The artists' entrance door slams shut behind him with a resounding thud.

"What the fuck," Tara exclaims. "We leave for Fresno in two hours."

"I'll get him, don't worry." Gabi stands up, trying to keep her composure. "I knew him before the army..." She lets out a small sigh. "I know it's the war that changed him. I feel like I'm the only one who knew him before, during, and after. He never talks about it," she says, her voice breaking. She gathers her things and heads out the back door to find Jake.

The silence that follows is heavy.

"We need someone reliable," Michelle insists. "Someone who can be there for us, for the music."

"I'll look into it," Tara says, her voice careful as she looks around the room, noticing each person's expression.

Gene nods. Carlos shifts uncomfortably. He glances around the room, taking in the somber faces of his friends. His heart pounds, anxiety and resolve battling for dominance. Then he hesitantly nods. "Yeah, it's time."

LATER THAT NIGHT, Carlos lies in bed, staring up at the smooth ceiling of his room. The space feels more lived in now, though the sparse furniture still gives it a sense of emptiness, especially without his drums here anymore. The outdated posters and decorations his parents put up when they first moved in are gone, replaced with photos of him and his friends. These images, capturing moments of laughter and connection, should bring comfort, but tonight they only remind him of how much has changed—and how much more might still need to change.

As he shifts under the covers, memories begin flashing through his mind—Jake's distant body language earlier tonight at the show in Fresno, mingling with memories of their early days, back when the band was just a dream and their friendship was less complicated. Carlos had been searching for another veteran with artistic ambitions, hoping to find someone who could relate to the unique challenges he faces. But now, those times seem far away, almost out of reach.

The photos on the wall catch his eye, the smiles frozen in time, reminding him that change is inevitable. Carlos feels the weight of the decisions ahead, knowing nothing can stay the same, no matter how much he might want it to. The room, now more in tune with his current life, also carries echoes of the past and the uncertainty of what lies ahead.

He takes a deep breath, hoping to find some peace in the steady rhythm of his breathing and the quiet of the room. But the photos—those frozen moments—keep pulling him back, making sleep elusive.

In an attempt to distract himself, he opens his laptop and starts watching a stand-up special; the noise helps to drown out the ringing in his ears and his racing thoughts. When sleep finally comes, it's restless, haunted by the same unanswered questions that will greet him with the dawn.

21

THE HORRIBLE PARTY

After their final show in Bakersfield, the band has planned a party at Jake's house to celebrate the upcoming tour. Jake's parents are visiting family across town, leaving Jake with the house, the pool, and the spacious backyard.

Carlos arrives and walks through the house toward the yard, guided by the sounds of the party already in full swing. As he steps outside, he spots Jake, who is visibly agitated. He sways slightly as he makes his way through the crowd, his eyes unfocused. Music blares, and people are scattered in and around the pool, which has clouds of smoke hovering and swirling above.

Carlos navigates through the unfamiliar faces, searching for Gabi, Gene, and Michelle while keeping an eye on Jake's behavior. A couple of women approach him, giggling.

"Hey, Carlos! Great show tonight," one of them says, batting her eyelashes.

"Thanks," Carlos replies with a brief smile, his eyes scanning the crowd. "Excuse me," he adds, spotting Gabi, Gene, and Michelle near the pool, surrounded by a small, enthusiastic crowd. He joins them, feeling a sense of relief to be among friends. "There you guys are." The four of them stay close, keeping an eye on the unfolding scene.

"Everyone, listen up!" Jake yells as he climbs onto the picnic table, knocking over a few drinks in the process. "I have something to say!" The small group around the table quiets down, turning their attention to Jake. The rest of the party continues obliviously, enjoying their own conversations. Carlos, Gabi, Gene, and Michelle exchange worried glances.

"You know what?" Jake continues. "This band... this band wouldn't exist without me! I started it! I named it! And what do I get in return?" He points accusingly at Gene and Michelle. "You two..." His voice fades for a moment. "It's not fair..."

"Jake, come down from there. You're drunk," Gabi pleads.

"No, I'm not. This is my second beer."

"Jake, we appreciate you. You're a vital part of the band. Come down, let's talk about this," Carlos says, calmly trying to defuse the situation.

"Why are you making a scene?" Gabi continues. "You need to stop this. You're hurting yourself."

"Hurting myself? You think I don't know that? I've been hurting for a long time, Gabi. And no one cares," Jake laments.

"Whatever. So now you're drinking? That's so stupid."

"Oh, come on. And stop critiquing me all the time. That's like half our interactions now. It's fucking obnoxious."

"What are we doing?" Gabi sighs as Michelle pulls on her arm to leave.

"Hold on a sec, Michelle. What do you mean, 'What are we doing?'" he booms at Gabi as he jumps off the table.

"I mean what the fuck is happening to you?"

"Oh fuck off," he shouts. With that, he storms off toward the house, leaving a stunned silence in his wake. Gabi, tears in her eyes, looks at Carlos, Gene, and Michelle.

"That's it. He's out of the band tonight. It's time to pull the trigger," Michelle says.

"Agreed," says Gene. The three look at Carlos.

"Yeah, it's time," Carlos mumbles after a pause. The band members exchange a solemn nod, realizing the gravity of their decision.

"Let's do it," Gene says as Jake stalks out into the backyard again and comes toward them with unresolved words on his face. Before Jake can come close or say anything, Michelle puts her arm up to stop him.

"You're out of the band," she says firmly. Gene moves to stand next to Michelle.

They all look at Carlos, who's still standing between Jake and the rest of the band.

"So you agree? Are you with them?" Jake's voice is sharp, laced with betrayal.

Carlos hesitates, feeling the weight of what he's about to do. He glances at Jake, the echo of their shared past and shared dreams in his mind. But he begins moving toward Gene and Michelle, drawn to the quiet understanding in Gene's eyes and Michelle's calm strength. The distance between him and Jake grows with each step. Carlos reaches Gene and Michelle, his choice now clear.

"Yes," he says, the word carrying more than just his decision.

Jake's eyes widen in disbelief, then narrow in rage. "Fuck you, too, then. You pussy. And a Purple Heart just means you weren't paying attention." The venom in his words stings, but Carlos stands his ground.

They all turn and leave Jake standing there alone amongst the party-goers.

"You too, Gabi?" he calls after her.

She stops, glancing back. "Didn't you tell me to fuck off?" she says before walking away.

.   .   .

OUT FRONT, Michelle leans against her car, keys dangling from her fingers. "Anyone need a ride home?" she asks, scanning their tired faces. Carlos glances at her, raising his eyebrows.

A small smile tugs at her lips. "When would I have had the time to get drunk?"

The group chuckles. One by one, they climb into her car, a mix of relief and weariness in their movements. Carlos slides into the back, leaning his head against the window.

They pull away from the curb, the city lights blurring into a steady stream. Inside the car, the silence grows, broken only by the soft hum of the tires on the road and the rhythm of the turn signals. Carlos watches the passing lights, feeling the quiet weight of the night settle over him. Michelle's hands grip the wheel with calm determination, her focus unwavering.

When they arrive at Gabi's house, Michelle parks the car and spins her head around, her eyes earnest. Gabi, sitting beside Carlos, nudges his arm gently, her voice soft yet insistent. "Come inside with me," she says. He pauses, letting the quiet of the car seep in, then nods.

He follows her to the door, the night air warm against his skin. Gene and Michelle exchange a knowing glance, offering a brief wave before driving away, leaving Carlos and Gabi at the doorstep.

Inside, Gabi's house feels cozy. The living room is dimly lit, with soft music playing in the background. Carlos feels nervousness adorned with excitement as Gabi leads him to the couch.

"Wanna smoke?" she asks, holding up a small tin.

"Sure," he replies, trying to steady his racing heart.

They sit down, a comfortable silence settling between them as Gabi lights up a joint and takes a hit before passing it to Carlos. The familiar scent of weed fills the room, easing some of the tension.

"So, crazy night, huh?" Gabi asks, leaning back into the cushions.

Carlos exhales slowly, feeling the calm wash over him. "Yeah," he laughs. "I can't believe we went through with it. It's all happening so fast."

Gabi nods, her eyes thoughtful. "Yeah, it's a big move. But you guys are ready. I've seen how hard you've worked."

Carlos smiles. "Thanks, Gabi." He pauses, pulse racing. "So, what does this mean for you and Jake?"

"I'm done."

"Fuck, that sucks. I'm sorry..."

"Honestly, I still have love for him, but I'm not in love anymore."

"I wonder if he'll remember what happened."

"I'll call him tomorrow."

She shifts closer, her eyes meeting his. She runs her hand through his curls. "Your hair is getting so long. I can't see your ears anymore."

Carlos gazes at her, appreciating the sincerity in her eyes. "Yeah, I know. I haven't cut it at all since we were in Kuwait."

"It looks good now," she teases.

Gabi's hand brushes against his, lingering just a moment longer than necessary. He notices how her warm, almond-shaped eyes soften when she looks at him, how her body relaxes as they talk, her long, thick hair draped over one of her shoulders. His heart beats a little faster, his words coming out more freely.

Gabi's gaze drifts to Carlos's scarred hand. Her fingers lightly trace the edges of the rough skin. Carlos stiffens for a moment, then relaxes, a small smile playing on his lips.

The space between them seems to shrink on its own, like an invisible force drawing them closer. Their voices become hushed, their words turning into whispers meant just for them.

Gabi leans in, her lips brushing his in a tentative kiss.

Carlos responds, his hands finding their way to her waist. The night deepens as they explore this new connection, their worries and the world outside fading away.

JAKE KICKS an empty beer can out of his path as the party winds down. Most of the guests have left, leaving only a few stragglers and the cokeheads who won't stop talking long enough to notice the house emptying. Eventually, even they take off, leaving Jake with just two new friends. They stumble to the kitchen, laughing as they rummage through the fridge for snacks.

Feeling restless, Jake leaves them and heads outside to the pool. He strips down to his boxers and lies on the third step, the cool water up to his chest and his legs stretched out and crossed in front of him. He sets his beer on the edge of the pool and leans back, his head resting near his drink. The night is calm and warm, the stars above in clear opposition to the chaos of the night.

The weight of the evening's events bear down on him, and the mixture of pills and alcohol makes him drowsy. His eyelids droop, and before he realizes it, he falls asleep. His head slips under the water, and his body slowly rolls down the steps.

Back in the kitchen, his new friends have settled on their snacks and are eating on the island. They chat casually, the kitchen filled with the sound of their laughter and clashing dishes.

22

THE TERRIBLE NEWS

"So, we all agree that moving forward with Rhys is the best step for the band?" Tara begins, her voice steady but soft as she makes eye contact with each band member gathered in the empty rehearsal space. "He's learned the set already."

"Damn, that was fast," Gene says, impressed.

Tara nods. "Yeah, I'd say he's dedicated," she laughs. "He's also excited to join us. He'll be at the next rehearsal." She looks at the pile of guitar and drum cases stacked on the stage. "Which reminds me, we gotta move this gear out of here today."

"Let's go!" Michelle shouts.

Carlos leans back in his chair, feeling a weight lifting off his shoulders. The tension that Jake brought to every rehearsal had been suffocating. He looks around at his bandmates, noting the same relief mirrored in their expressions.

Michelle glances at Carlos, a spark of enthusiasm in her eyes. "I've already started reworking some of the songs with the new guitar parts. It's gonna sound incredible."

Gene grins. "Can't wait to hear it."

Carlos nods, feeling a renewed sense of purpose. "Here's to a fresh start."

Tara smiles, the tension in the room dissolving into a collective optimism. "Alright, let's get to work. We have a lot to prepare for, and I know we're gonna kill it."

As the band discusses logistics and schedules, Carlos's phone buzzes insistently in his pocket. It's Gabi. Excusing himself, he steps outside to take the call. Gene watches him go, making kissing noises.

Minutes later, Carlos re-enters the room, his expression altered—pale, shaken. The room falls silent, all eyes on him as he struggles to find the words.

"Jake's dead," he finally manages. The words sound foreign in the quiet room. "He drowned last night."

Michelle's eyes widen, disbelief evident. "What?"

"How?" Gene jumps up, nearly knocking over his chair.

Carlos takes a shaky breath. "Yeah, I guess he drowned in the pool after we all left. His parents came home this morning and found him."

"What the fuck," Gene mutters, his voice thick with shock.

Carlos's eyes drift downward, his voice barely above a whisper. "Apparently, his parents also found a couple of people passed out in the living room, oblivious. I was oblivious... I should've stayed."

The room's atmosphere shifts, the air dense with an overwhelming mix of sorrow, guilt, and disbelief. Shock hits them like a tidal wave, leaving them breathless and reeling.

"I'm so sorry," Tara says softly, her role as manager momentarily giving way to her concern as a friend.

They all remain in silence for a few minutes, the quiet atmosphere almost worse than the news. Carlos looks at the stage, where their gear is stacked neatly in piles of cases. He glances over and sees Michelle and Gene doing the same, their eyes glossed over and unblinking.

"Fuck," Michelle says, breaking the silence as she drops her head into her hands. Gene walks over and places a hand on her shoulder.

"Now what?" Carlos says under his breath, as if just speaking to himself.

The room gradually quiets again, the weight of Jake's absence settling over them like a heavy fog. Tara clears her throat, breaking the silence. "We need to talk about what comes next," she says softly, her eyes moving between the remaining members. "Not about Rhys. We got that. But... about Jake..."

Michelle is quiet, staring at the floor as if searching for answers in the worn-out concrete. "Jake wasn't just another musician," she finally says, her voice low. "He was our friend. Whatever we do next, it has to be something he would've wanted..."

"His face on the album cover?" Gene attempts to joke, then sighs, his expression solemn as he sits back down.

Carlos sits up a little straighter, the responsibility settling on his shoulders. "Well, we gotta dedicate our first performance of the tour to him," he suggests. "At the very least. Our way of saying goodbye... and making sure his legacy stays with the band."

"Totally," Michelle nods.

Gene finally looks up, meeting Carlos's eyes. "He was... complicated, but he was one of us."

They end the meeting and the bandmates come together in a tearful group hug, their foreheads resting on each other like a tripod. Tara walks over and places a hand on Carlos's back. With heavy hearts, they remove their gear from the stage for good, marking the end of an era.

EVERYONE LEAVES the basement except Carlos. He stays seated, staring at the bare stage. The empty room echoes with the sounds of their practice, a haunting reminder of the band's struggles and successes.

He hears footsteps, and then Gabi appears on the staircase to the right of the stage. "Did everyone leave?" she asks, breathless, her steps and voice cutting through the silence.

"Yeah, you just missed them," Carlos replies, still fixated.

"Oh. Well, you were the one I wanted to see. How are you feeling about all this?" Her eyes linger on Carlos, worry and grief etched in her expression.

Carlos finally looks at her. "Me? What about *you*?"

"I keep waiting for the deep sadness, but I'm like, numb," she says, joining Carlos in the seat next to him, her head resting in her hands.

"Don't worry, it's just delayed. The human body has some weird defense mechanisms," Carlos says, gently resting a hand on her shoulder.

"I hate that you know that."

"Rhys... He's learned the set already," Carlos adds, his arm returning to his knees as he leans forward.

"This is all too fast." Gabi's voice wavers, her posture tense. "I should have stayed."

"I thought the same..." Carlos's voice trails off. Seeing Gabi's unease, he wonders if she feels as guilty as he does. "Don't hold it in when the flood comes."

"How are *you*, though?" Gabi's eyes search his face.

Carlos hesitates, his gaze dropping to the floor. "I mean..." He laughs, but the sound is hollow, devoid of joy.

"You always laugh when things are bad. Makes me feel better," Gabi says softly. "I'm gonna miss that."

"Wait, what? What do you mean?" Carlos asks, apprehension in his voice. His eyes dart to hers, searching for clarity.

"I found out this morning after you left that I got accepted to NYU."

"Wow, congrats." Carlos tries to sound enthusiastic, but his heart sinks.

"Thanks."

"So, you're leaving." The weight of the realization settles over him.

"Yeah..."

"Wow..." His voice fades. "Now what?"

"You guys are in good hands with Tara and the label."

"That's not what I meant."

Gabi opens her mouth to speak but stops herself. Her eyes turn to the floor.

They sit in silence for a moment, unspoken words hanging between them. Carlos glances at the empty stage again, his thoughts a jumbled mess. He feels a knot tighten in his chest. Gabi shifts next to him, her presence a mix of comfort and heartache.

He runs his scarred hand through his hair, steadying his emotions. The room starts to feel lighter, filled with the ringing of their past conversations. He looks at Gabi, noticing the mix of curiosity and guilt in her face as she looks at him.

"I guess I always knew you'd leave eventually," he says, finally showing a small smile. "Weird to say at a time like this, but... I'm proud of you."

"Thank you." Gabi spins toward him. "I'm done with Bakersfield. There's never gonna be a better time for me to move on. It's funny; this morning I was contemplating whether I should tell you or Jake the news first. Then his mom called me..."

"Well, don't let me stop you."

"Thanks for your permission," she says dryly, making Carlos laugh and shake his head.

He glances at the stage, a quiet reminder of how music has helped him heal, then sits up and slaps his hands on his knees, a newfound confidence radiating from him despite the lingering shadow of pain in his eyes. He lets out a deep breath, a mix of resignation and acceptance washing over him.

"Well, fuck," he says, a small, wry grin playing on his lips as he looks back at Gabi. "Timing sucks, doesn't it?"

ACKNOWLEDGMENTS

Writing *The Horrible Terribles* has been an unforgettable journey, and it would not have been possible without the support, guidance, and encouragement of several remarkable people.

To my mom, dad, brother, and my son, thank you for your unwavering support, patience, and love throughout this process. You have always been there, even when I wasn't sure where this path would lead.

To my editors, Jaime Johns and Madeleine Swart, your insights and feedback helped shape this book into what it is today. Your attention to detail and understanding of my vision allowed me to dig deeper and make every word count.

To my friends, especially those who listened to my endless drafts and brainstorms, thank you for your honesty and enthusiasm. Your input not only inspired new ideas but also kept me grounded.

To my fellow artists and creators, particularly those in the Bakersfield and Los Angeles communities, your dedication to your craft has been a constant source of motivation.

To past and present veterans, thank you for your service and sacrifices. Your stories, experiences, and resilience have been an inspiration, and this book would not be what it is without your example.

Finally, to the readers, I thank you from the bottom of my heart. You make this journey worth it.

ABOUT THE AUTHOR

Diego Barrientos was born in Guatemala City, Guatemala, and raised in California's San Joaquin Valley. After graduating high school, he enlisted in the U.S. Army and was deployed to the Iraq War. Upon returning, Diego pursued his life-long passion for music, playing drums in bands such as Vogue in the Movement and The New Post before transitioning to visual arts. He earned his MFA in Fine Art from the California Institute of the Arts.

Diego's work has been featured at the Institute of Contemporary Art, Los Angeles, and in various galleries throughout Southern California. Now based in Los Angeles, he is a painter, fiction writer, graphic designer, and multi-instrumentalist. His artistic practice draws on his diverse experiences, weaving together visual storytelling with a deep connection to music and cultural influences.

instagram.com/dee.barrientos

youtube.com/@dangerouspenguinproductions